19.00

ONE WAY TO HEAVEN

AMS PRESS
NEW YORK

ONE WAY
TO HEAVEN

by

Countee Cullen

Harper & Brothers Publishers
New York and London
1 9 3 2

Library of Congress Cataloging in Publication Data

Cullen Countee, 1903-1946.
One way to heaven.

Reprint of the ed. published by Harper, New York.
I. Title.
PZ3.C897610n7   [PS3505.U287]   813'.5'2   73-18572
ISBN 0-404-11383-4

Reprinted by arrangement with Harper & Row, Publishers, Inc.

From the edition of 1932, New York and London
First AMS edition published in 1975
Manufactured in the United States of America

AMS PRESS INC.
NEW YORK, N. Y. 10003

For

HAROLD JACKMAN

ONE WAY TO HEAVEN

PART ONE

Note

*Some of the characters
in this book are
fictitious*

*

Chapter One

SAM LUCAS, striding through the raw, mor-
dant December night felt that he had chosen
an ill moment in which to come to Harlem. New
York was bright and gay, and these colored people
looked happy, as he had been told he would find
them; but they also seemed too intent upon their
own affairs to promise much attention to an ill-
starred stranger. Their faces did not radiate that
hospitality which he had left behind in the south-
land. He had been years getting here, dallying on
the way, making love and turning tricks, settling
here and there for a month or two, or a year, but
with his eyes and his heart set more lover-like on
New York than they had ever been set on a woman.
Time and time again he had unloosed himself
from the tightening knots of an embrace and had
set his feet on the one way he felt he had to go.
He had begged rides in wagons and trucks from
town to town (it was a long way up from Texas) ;
he had swung on to freighters and would bear
their mark upon him till he died. It was over six
years now since he had lost his left arm when,

clambering down to escape detection, he had missed his footing and had fallen, with his arm stretched out like an enticement for the sharp rear wheel that had kissed him into unconsciousness. Ever after he had had a feeling of having been buried before his time.

He drew his frayed overcoat more closely about his lean, rawboned body, and tucked his armless left sleeve into his pocket where it would not flap in the wind. Shivering, he quickened the speed of his gaunt, limber legs, and buried his face down into the confines of his coat collar, letting his own breath rise steaming up to warm his neck and ears. He had a fine, intelligent-looking face which he could never justify with his mind; a slightly elongated head with high-mounting cheek-bones, and sinking jaws, which gave him a hungry, somewhat acidulous look though his stomach might be full and satisfied; he often wondered why his mouth should be so wide and his lips so thin; he sometimes pursed his mouth up when he laughed, ashamed of its reckless expanse whenever he happened to let himself go; but he was proud of his strong, even white teeth, wedged like unpunctured dice in their firm red sockets. He had a woman's conceit for his eyes and his skin. The former were a deep electric brown, and nothing could be blacker or smoother than his skin, marred only where a long knife-wound in healing had left a sweeping streak of tan on one cheek, like a filament of brown hair imbedded in jet.

Suddenly he stopped before a mammoth pile of brown stone which by means of a gilt-and-black signboard proclaimed itself the Mount Hebron African Methodist Episcopal Church. Sam whistled long and loudly as he gazed at it, thinking, "My people sure are rising." Various placards tacked to the ecclesiastical doors or tied to the iron railing which ran along outside the church announced that watch-night services were being held, and that the Reverend Clarence Johnson, a famed singing evangelist from Texas, would preach the last sermon of the old year.

He joined the deepening stream of people entering the church, and as he stood on the threshold, letting his eyes roam for a moment over the vast auditorium, he sensed an involuntary thrill of satisfaction and self-commendation course through him, as though he were contemplating a thing of his own creating. Here he was in the largest Negro church in New York City on watch night. He could not escape the wonder of it. Shaped like a half-moon, the huge auditorium groaned beneath its mingled weight of the righteous and the unregenerate. Every bit of space into which a body could be squeezed with any degree of discomfort, had been utilized. In happy Christian violation of the laws of health and fire-prevention, small, collapsible camp chairs had been placed in the aisles. There would be no such crowd as this again until Easter Sunday morning; the seasons between the celebration of the birth and death of Christ were always slack; only on watch night and at Easter time was the real power of the church flashed forth beyond the range of doubt; only then like some granite octopus did its many doors reach out and suck in to utter satiation. For throughout the year good luck follows him who is found in the house of the Lord when New Year's chimes are sounded; and on Easter Sunday, if it is bright and sunny, church attendance is as happy a prelude to Harlem's fashion parade as to that of lower Fifth Avenue.

Sam managed to squeeze into one of the forward pews, where, after divesting himself of his overcoat, he sat cramped and uncomfortable between a meek-looking brown man and an obese saffron-hued woman who, despite the energy with which she was helping to sing "You must be a lover of the Lord," frankly resented his intrusion, showing her displeasure by singing more loudly and more off key. He flashed the hot electric current of his eyes upon her and let his smile go, not caring into how wide a grin his thin lips might stretch; that smile, he knew, at its best was irresistible. His neighbor capitulated, and withdrew some of her bulk into herself in order to give him a bit more room.

He settled himself, and sat back in a reverie, his heavy black lids drooping down and stemming the bright dynamic flow of his eyes. He let his right hand glide slowly and gently into the pocket of his jacket with a movement at once both searching and caressing, as if he sought to assure himself that something cherished and serviceable was in its accustomed place. An easy, satisfied smile grew and spread over his countenance as his hand encountered the desired object. The smile vanished as suddenly as it had appeared while his hand stroked something in his pocket with the gentle back-and-forth motion with which one might stroke a small and frightened kitten, hoping to ease it of its fear.

He was biding his time. Inside he felt interchangeably hot and cold, and his stomach seemed to recede from him, hollow and sunken, making him feel as though he were falling from a great height. It was always like that when he entered a church intent on giving a performance. Tonight's setting filled him with pride; the immensity of the place, the number of the people, appalled and fascinated him. On this evening's program he felt that he was to play a particular and enviable part, a rôle not to be exceeded even by that of the Reverend Clarence Johnson, whose importation from Texas was there on the outside in large black letters for all to see. *He* had not been sent for, but he too was a powerful instrument in the hands of the Lord. His rôle called for no particular cue; he was his own cue-master. Over a period of eight years he had played this part in twelve states, and hoped before he died to play them all.

It was testimonial time. All around him people were rising, singing, talking, testifying, telling what the Lord had done for them throughout the year, some saying that times had been bad, that adversity and sickness and death had tracked them down, but that when they lay pinned to the earth and gasping for breath, the Lord God Jehovah had reached down and raised them up. Their faces, for the most part, were animated with a sincere fervor that seemed to run from one to another, although here and there were persons who spoke in voices listlessly unintonated, as if they were speaking pieces the import of which was totally lost to them. Many prefaced their testimonials with hymns, some in gayly syncopated time that made their hands and the listeners' rush together impulsively, measures that careened through the body, setting their feet tapping and stretching

their mouths wide with loud hosannas and amens;
while others sang tunes that were sorrowful and
heart-disturbing, as if the singers bore the weight
of the world upon their shoulders, as if the cross
were a very near and personal thing of which they
could not rid themselves, nor cared to; as if their
very happiness depended upon this very sorrow.

Their testimonials were repetitious and rich in
homely similes.

"I've put my hand to the gospel-plow, and I
can't let go till my harvest comes." The speaker,
a tall Indian-looking woman with a beaked nose
advancing from a proud, stern face, lifted her
hand as she spoke, as if calling upon the elements
to witness the unshakableness of her decision.

"I'm clinging to the old rugged cross." This
time it was a man, short, squat, thick-set, his yellow
face marked strongly with Asiatic crossings, his
short hair curled and rebellious. "I'm climbing
the rough side of the mountain," he continued,
plaintively, "but Jesus holds me by the hand."

As if the picture were more than he could bear,
a young boy seated behind the testifier sniggered
outright, and then stuffed his handkerchief into
his mouth in a vain attempt to marshal himself
into proper church behavior.

Midway of the church a small child stood up
and quoted, "Jesus wept." A faint wave of laugh-

ter, like a soft wind touching grass, rippled across the church, and died, caught up and lost in the sober realization that God's house was not a place for levity.

There were those who declared with conviction, "I know that my Redeemer liveth," and then sat down with proud, radiant faces. Others simply importuned, "Pray for me," and took their seats shyly, as if confused, like neophytes who were embarrassed in the presence of those whose church membership was longer, whose religious experience was wider. And many combined both prayer and promise, saying, "Pray for me, and on the judgment morning I'll be there to help crown Him Lord of all."

At length when, in their anxiety to testify, dozens of people rose simultaneously from their seats, each endeavoring to be heard above his neighbor's equally futile but valiant attempts, the local preacher, a small, dark man who was conducting this phase of the service, raised his hand, interposing silence.

"This has been beautiful," he said, stretching his hands forth as if he would draw the entire church to him, and bless them. "The Lord has been here and walked among us. We have felt the wind from His garments blow upon us as He passed by. But some of us haven't been able to speak for Him, and it's now time for our preaching. It's eleven o'clock. One more hour and the old year will be gone. I am going to ask all those who haven't testified and who do love the Lord, and you're trying to walk in the way you feel He'd want you to go, just to rise silently and so express your desire to press onward to the higher mark which is in Christ Jesus."

Half the congregation rose and stood silent with bowed heads for a few moments, and then sat down. Of those who had remained seated, not all had testified; some were brazen, unrepentant, untouched. Sam Lucas had not testified, nor did he stand.

A door which gave off from the rostrum opened; two men came out and mounted into the pulpit. The first, the Reverend Mr. Drummond, pastor of Mount Hebron Church, was a thick-set tannish man with exaggerated eyebrows and a copious mustache. His walk was deliberate; his eyes were hazy and gentle. He wasted no time, but walked directly to the lectern, where he proclaimed in a voice so deep that his words issued from his cavernous mouth like growls, "We are glad to have with us tonight our brother in the gospel, Reverend Clarence Johnson, who has come to us all the way from Texas, to break to us the bread of life. All you who know the worth of prayer, pray with him, that what he says may be to the good of our souls and to the glory of God."

Bible in ‹hand, Reverend Johnson advanced, singing. He was slight of build, yet with a slenderness that suggested a dormant vitality; his eyes were bright and hard; they betokened temper and a zealousness unwedded to an equivalent patience. When he moved, he gave the impression that somewhere behind him, or above him, were invisible strings held by steady hands which compelled his movements. His voice was a surprise; for seeing him enter one felt that he was vocally unequipped to send a message into the recesses of that vast tabernacle. But as he sang, his voice went out in rich, clearly-accentuated waves of melody, as if he somehow had managed to reach down and press upward into his throat all the blood and vigor which coursed through his body.

> "I've opened my mouth to the Lord,
> And I won't turn back;
> I will go, I shall go
> To see what the end will be."

It was a good tune, well chosen; it was warm, irresistible to throat and hands and feet, the sort of song which those who didn't know the words hummed, to which bodies swayed in spiritual syncopation; a sturdy hymn which, when it ended,

would not die away in a gurgle, as if it had suddenly been throttled, but which would carry in
its wake a ripple of amens and hallelujahs. It was
elemental Negro religion expressing itself in song.

"I am the Resurrection and the Life."

He had chosen his text and was preaching. Here
was no treatise for the learned, no hairs to split for
quibblers; if there were doctors and lawyers and
school-teachers here tonight, if smart young college girls and boys had sauntered in, with horns
and cowbells hidden beneath their coats in readiness for the New Year's frenzy, there were also
simple, more naïve, unlettered people here who
were hungry for something which he could give
them. They wanted the five loaves and the two
fish. He had tried to lift his followers up to him
when he first started to preach, years ago, a raw,
young recruit, with advanced ideas and a fine
scorn for simplicity and unquestioning belief. But
long ago he had discovered that he must go down
to them. If he did not believe all he preached, if
sometimes he doubted the virgin birth of Christ
and the infinite wisdom of God, after having sent
mourners away shining with belief and satisfaction, he scourged himself with penitence, he
fasted and prayed, endeavoring to appease he knew
not what dreadful Who.

"I have given you these," he would cry; "help

my unbelief"; and he would go forth to preach again.

"I am the Resurrection and the Life." . . . The soaring, vibrant voice spoke on. He was no common preacher; he was an artist. There was fire enough in him to commit that truth to the most ignorant hearts before him. He need not make use of the four letters which with utter propriety might be strung behind his name, no more than he needed the two honor keys which he never wore, of which he never spoke, the exact location of which, were he asked, he could not tell. Such insignia he had discarded when he went down to the people, throwing them aside as weights which might too easily beset him. Those who came to him wanted poetry (though they might not have called it that) and song, and all the beaded, miraculous wine of the Bible. They came from the washtub, they came with hands calloused from mop and pail and skillet. They had no hunger for the hard bread of reason, but for the soft, easily digested manna of magic.

Slowly and graphically he depicted the betrayal and the crucifixion of Christ. He made each feel upon his own cheek the flame of the dastardly kiss, speaking with an intensity that caused many to look at their own hands, half fearing to find them red and raw with the marks of nails; for never had the blows of those far-off hammers been so dinned into their ears. When he spoke of the glory of the resurrection, they saw the three women wonder-stricken before the open tomb, at its side the great and ponderous stone rolled away; he recreated for them the angel standing with his sword of petrified fire; in the fervor of his narration, he gave the angel a name, numbered his wings to the count of six, and told what his specific duties were in heaven. He plied the wings of his imagination and floated away as if on a magic carpet.

And yet the fire did not fall. He had spoken half an hour and the fire had not burned. Here and there some one from time to time said, "Amen," or, "How true!" but for the most part his audience sat before him silent, attentive, but undemonstrative, a half-moon of faces, a rainbow of impassivity. He understood his people well enough to know that where there was no demonstration there was small success. He had hoped he would not be forced to resort to some things tonight. There were means of which he was weary. His most dependable tricks were frayed with use, dusty with time, yet powerful he knew through repetition. He had wanted to end on a note of joy and hope. But he must have the fire.

Now his walk became more spasmodic as he

strode the length of the pulpit; his voice grew menacing; his gestures snapped threats as though he were cracking an invisible whip at them. "I am the Resurrecton and the Life," he cried. "True, Christ *is* the resurrection and the life, but He is also death and everlasting damnation. To such as believe on Him He will give eternal life, rest in the bosom of Abraham, not only hereafter, but here. He will bind up your wounds, heal your broken hearts, pay your rent, supply food and clothing. But for such as reject Him He has prepared an horrible pit, a place of fire and brimstone, an everlasting hell. You liars, cheaters, whoremongers, where will you spend eternity? In peace with the sons of God, or thirsting in hell with Dives?"

Somewhere far back in the church a woman wailed. His face lighted up as an actor's at applause. With his open palm he smote the Bible before him; a sweeping gesture from his arm sent the lectern lamp to the floor, where the frosted bulb shattered into a small heap of snow-like glass. He was unaware of this calamity. The poet's frenzy and the prophet's power were upon him, and his meager frame trembled out of all control of brain or any restrictive muscle. At this moment he was pure emotion made man.

"Some of us," he reminded them, "have mothers

on the other side, and fathers, sisters and brothers and husbands and wives. We promised to meet them on the other side. Have we kept faith with them or have we lied to our dead? If any man sin, he has an Advocate in heaven. Who will place his case in Christ's hands? Earthly lawyers may fail you, but Christ has power before a tribunal greater than any on earth. He is the Captain who has never lost a battle, the Great Physician who has never lost a patient. His names are many and mighty. Some have called Him a little white stone cut out of the mountain, forever rolling and gathering strength. Some have said He was the Lily of the Valley, the Rose of Sharon, the Bright and Morning Star, the fairest among ten thousand. But I think the sweetest name He bears is Saviour. Who will come up before the old year goes out and the new year comes in, and let Him save you? Who will come, just as you are?"

His face was shining, anxious, glowing with sweat. He began to sing:

> "Just as I am without one plea,
> But that Thy blood was shed for me,
> And that Thou bidst me come to Thee,
> O Lamb of God, I come, I come."

The church stirred clumsily like some mammoth shifting in slumber; as the tension relaxed into curiosity, heads were turned to see who would come forward; people looked at their neighbors accusingly, wondering why they did not go up and be saved. The hymn droned on, slow, sluggish, literary. A young girl circled the entire church, groped along the walls, and finally reached the pulpit, where she knelt down and hid her face in her hands. A man shuffled down the mid-aisle and knelt beside her.

But that fire which consumes did not fall. Fifteen minutes to the new year. The hymn slid forward into silence, lost on a pathetic note of defeat.

"Who will come? Who will change his way of living?

"If I were you I'd make a change,
    If I were you I'd make a change,
    If I were you I'd make a change,
    Oh, my friend, can't you hear God calling,
    Won't you make a change?"

He had come down from the rostrum, and now he stood within the little railing that encircled the lower pulpit. As he sang he held his hands extended toward them, pleading. This new song was something of his own, an invitation which he had created for their need. They understood it, caught it up, swayed to it, paid it lusty tribute with hands and feet. The tempo was lively; with different words and sung a bit more slowly it would have answered admirably as a blues. There was native sorrow in it, and native wit:

"O dancing girl, won't you make a change?"

In the gallery a woman screamed, threw back her head, and beat the air about her, until two women ushers, ample parcels of womanhood that might have been selected for just this purpose, rushed up and held her; they stationed themselves at her sides, pinioned her arms firmly, and let her leap up and down between them as if she were jumping a rope. From time to time as she jumped she cried, "Sweet Jesus." A spare man with aqueous blue eyes set in a sullen, fair face walked up to the altar with a defiant stride, and knelt down, while the thin little brown woman who had been sitting with him ran down the aisle behind him, caught him to her breast, and cried out for all the church to hear, "I thank you, Jesus, I thank you," and then went back to her seat.

The fire was burning now; like a natural man the Holy Ghost was walking among them. Reverend Johnson's eyes were kindled with the zeal of the proselyter. He strode back and forth within the altar rail, letting his hand rest for a moment on each of the heads bowed down before him, whispering to each penitent some word of comfort or some promise:

"If you make one step, my brother, Christ will make two.

"Though your sins be as scarlet, my sister, believe on Him, and they shall be whiter than snow.

"Come without money, sister; come buy and eat; come eat of the tree of life, and drink from the fountain that never shall run dry."

Seven more minutes to the new year, and he had but three mourners there before him. He looked over his audience and saw, not far from him, a withered yellow woman pleading vigorously with a young girl seated at her side. From where he stood he could see that the girl was pretty; the string of flashy red beads that circled her throat lighted up her black face like sunshine on black satin. Her black hat was edged with red, and her lips, pressed tightly and sullenly together, glowed more brightly than he felt they should. He had no reason to, but he thought of Mary Magdelene, and he felt that this woman would be a welcome sacrifice on the altar of the Lord, a tribute which would be taken up in smoke and flames like the venison of Abel. He would go down to her.

The faded yellow woman at her side saw him coming and settled back in her seat to leave the matter in more persuasive hands. He bent over the girl and whispered:

"Are you a Christian, my child?"

She turned dark, resentful eyes on him, and he felt suddenly that even for the Lord's sake he should not have intruded upon her.

"No, I'm not," she said.

"Then why don't you become one tonight? Why don't you change now and become one of God's children? Come, let us pray for you."

She would not answer him, but stared straight ahead of her, and sheer through her smooth even-coated blackness he could see the flush of embarrassment rise up and flood her face.

"Won't you come, my sister?"

A stubborn man himself, he recognized intractability when he encountered it, and so turned away from her at last, ashamed and beaten.

His heart was hot within him; he felt undone and cheated as he walked back to the altar rail; not even the three mourners abjectly curved there could lighten him; he could have passed them all by for that vital arrow-slim figure in red and black which had rejected all the blandishments of the Lord. He felt personally humiliated. Though there were ninety and nine safely penned into the fold, he keenly coveted this one stray sheep. As he sensed a familiar warmth inundate his cheeks, he cooled them with a brutal, angry stroke from the back of his hand.

And then Sam Lucas and the devil stepped in.

"O mother's son, won't you make a change.
O mother's son, won't you make a change,
O mother's son, won't you make a change,
O mother's son, don't you hear God calling,
Won't you make a change?"

While the church rocked gently back and forth to this verse, Sam rose from his seat and squeezed past the three persons between him and the aisle. His stout neighbor encouraged him with, "Lord help you, son." Tears welled in his eyes, overflowed them, and trickled down his cheeks. He had half the church to traverse in order to reach the mourner's bench. As he walked his left sleeve flapped. People became aware of this physical deficiency, and he could feel their pity flow out and engulf him. Reverend Johnson saw him coming, and his heart gladdened until his face shone.

As Sam reached the rail, he delved into his right-hand coat pocket, threw down something, then knelt down and sobbed.

The evangelist had started toward him, his hand pulsing with a benediction, his tongue a quiver brimming with arrows of consolation. But as he looked down and saw what lay at Sam's feet his hand recoiled as if controlled by a spring; his eyes congealed into pin-points of anger. There at his feet, spread out like a various-colored fan, was a pack of cards, and beside the cards, open and flashing with a sinister defiance, a bright razor.

"This man," the Reverend Johnson commenced in a voice so loud and troubled that Sam looked up in amazement which verged into a half-fearful recognition—"This man ——" but his words were lost in the tide of emotion which surged from the altar rail into lower pews and gallery; women wept and clapped their hands, men stomped and shouted. Here was magic which not even the preacher had been able to deal out to them: fifty-two playing-cards, a sharp bright razor, and a sinner's heart all displayed on the altar of the Lord. The very devil had been laid low before them.

"This man ——" the Reverend Johnson cried again, and was heard as much as one raindrop among thousands. He looked out over his audience and saw, with wonder tinged with resentment, the dark girl gazing with fascinated eyes on Sam's betrayed instruments of sin. She watched them for a moment, then rose slowly from her seat, wringing her hands. She took her head in her hands and rocked it back and forth, moaning, making soft unintelligible sounds like a hunted animal, wounded and too terror-stricken to cry

out lest it reveal its hiding-place. Reverend Johnson forgot what he had to say. He held out his
hands to her, and she rushed sobbing up to the
rail, where she knelt down beside Sam. Sam looked
at her through the slits between his fingers and
saw that she was pretty. In her wake eight other
persons came to the altar.

Like a man swaying on the edge of a dream,
Reverend Johnson knelt to pray. His voice
mounted over the congregation and quieted them:
"Lord, we thank thee for these many souls who
have come into Thy fold tonight. We pray Thy
guidance upon them throughout this coming year.
We ask that Thou wouldst strengthen their weakness, and make good Christians of them."

And then, as if something outside himself compelled him, he cried, "Thou movest in a mysterious way, Thy wonders to perform. Help us to
understand Thee. Amen."

Chapter Two

"What a happy New Year! What a happy New Year!"

THE congregation was standing now, singing over and over again, with loud happy voices the familiar words with which they annually greeted the incoming year, although its predecessor, welcomed in with the same sanguine spirit, might have done nothing so to confirm their renewed hopefulness. They were like chronic bargainers, people who buy diamonds and gold watches from strangers accosting them in the street, only to find that the diamonds are bits of stone, and the gold watches good, durable, odorous brass, and yet they continue to buy, hoping to encounter a real bargain in the end. Last year might have been lean, with little flour in the barrel, scant of clothing, an almost constant need of the doctor and his bitter doses, but this year, coming in with its hard, frosty weather, with sinners ready to mend the raveled fabric of their ways, with sinners and Christians both blowing horns and sounding bells in the street, this year would

surely be fat and prosperous. And so they sang
"What a happy New Year." They shook hands all
around. People who had never set eyes on one
another crossed aisles, leaned across benches,
threaded their way through other happy, grinning
groups, touched hands across other hands crossed
for a fitful second, and wished each other a Happy
New Year. Many wept and let the tears fall in unabashed contentment.

Even after Reverend Johnson had dismissed
them they seemed loth to go. They wanted to
shake the hands of the new converts and wish them
a long and faithful service in the house of the
Lord. They especially wanted to speak to Sam and
congratulate him; for his had been the most singular victory. Their lively imaginations had already
seized upon him and were fashioning legends
about him. Here was something they could display
when friends scoffed at religion. This man, with
his cards and his razor, had probably sauntered
into the church filled with derision, or moved by
some memory of his childhood which had said it
was good to be in the church when the new year
came. And he had been struck in the forehead,
straight between the eyes, with the words that the
preacher had flung against him, just as David,
balancing himself on one foot, had let go his
smooth little pebble straight into the mocking

height of "Golia." That velvety streak which a knife-wound had left on Sam's face, and the imperfection of his empty sleeve, made them think of dark and sinful doings, gambling and drinking and fighting. He was mystery and miracle and the confirmation of faith to them. They wondered how he had felt when the Spirit struck him, whether he had heard voices or seen resplendent shapes guiding him toward the altar. They were grateful to him, and as always there were some who showed their gratitude in the way on which Sam always counted. He hadn't lost his arm for nothing. Many, as they came up to shake hands with him, left a bill or a silver coin in his hand as they withdrew their own. Sam looked hurt as they did this, but grateful; he was too kind to offend them by a refusal.

The cards and the razor still lay on the floor. He bent to pick them up, but the Reverend Johnson stooped down before him, gathered up the trampled pack and the shining blade, saying: "Son, let me have these. I should like to keep them to remember this evening by."

Sam grinned. "Sure, preacher," but he had a growing feeling that perhaps the Reverend Johnson had said these same words to him somewhere else at some other time. And he thought, "I'll have to buy another deck and a new razor."

The church had thinned out now; only Sam, the Reverend Johnson, the Reverend Drummond, the dark girl in the red-and-black hat, and the faded yellow woman who had come with her, remained at the altar. The sextons, anxious to get home, began flashing the lights on and off in order to convey their readiness to these stragglers. Sam's pocket was heavy with silver, and he too wanted to leave, but something held him back. He was waiting for some move from the Reverend Johnson.

The dark girl came over to him and held out her hand. He took it and found that it was small, and not too rough in the palm. The back of the hand was smooth and cool.

"I want to thank you for what you did for me tonight," she said. "Oh, I'd like to talk to you and tell you what I feel. Which way are you going? Couldn't we walk along together?"

Next to getting religion and making it pay, Sam hankered after women; he aimed to impress them, he liked to feel that he had a way with them. He had never joined church yet but it had led to an affair. As lightly as he had taken his religion he had taken his women, and as often.

He looked at her, seeing her well and fully for the first time. She was black, not dull like pitch, but bright like jet. Her mouth was red and inviting. It was half-open now, and her teeth looked sound and clean. Her hair was straightened, no doubt, but he didn't mind that; he liked black women best. He would put her age at about twenty, no more than twenty-two. Her breasts made a hard, firm outline under her frock.

He smiled at her and said, "We can go any way you say, lady."

Reverend Johnson interposed here.

"I want to speak to this brother alone for a few minutes," he said, and his voice was like a vise. Sam felt it might be embarrassing to refuse.

"Sure thing," he growled.

The Reverend Drummond said: "You can take him into my study, and then leave by the back way. I'm tired, so I think I'll leave you." Looking at Sam, he warned, "I'll look to see you Sunday, brother, so that you can be taken in as a regular and full member with us." And to the girl, "You too, miss."

The girl said: "I'll wait here while you two talk, and when you're ready to go, you can call me. Then we can talk, Mr.—Mr. ——"

"Lucas, lady. Sam Lucas."

"Mr. Lucas, then."

Turning to the yellow woman with her, she patted her and drew her coat up about her, saying: "You'd best not wait for me, Aunt Mandy. You just go along, and I'll catch up with you later."

Her aunt squeezed her: "All right, honey. I'm so glad you done joined church at last, I could plumb shout all over again." She went up to Sam and took his hand, "Son, I ought to thank you, too, 'cause my Mattie here joined church when she saw you standing there with them cards and that razor laying at your feet. Let me go 'long now, or I'll sure be shouting again."

Sam followed the evangelist into Reverend Drummond's study. The preacher switched on a light, closed the door behind him, and motioned Sam to a seat. Sam slumped down into a chair at the end of a long table around which the church council probably held its monthly meetings. The evangelist took a seat at the other end. For a moment his hard, lively eyes beat sardonically into Sam's own, downing their effrontery. Sam let his eyes fall, knowing contention was useless. If this had been a woman facing him, he could have let the pure current of his own seeing flow out and conquer her.

Reverend Johnson beat a nervous staccato tatoo on the table; on his forehead and on the backs of his hands the veins stood out, faint blue streaks almost imperceptible beneath their tan covering.

At last he spoke, his voice wavering on the border line of contempt and reverence: "I am not sure that you are not the most despicable man I've ever come across; I'm not sure that you aren't a genius in your way, and I'm far from being certain that you aren't an unwitting instrument in the hands of Heaven."

Sam was confused by so much uncertainty; the word despicable was new to him; yet he had felt its thrust and had bristled instinctively, but he felt the compliment behind the evangelist's misgivings.

Indeed, he was so relieved that he permitted himself a smile, letting his mouth widen until the lips were stretched taut.

"Meaning what, preacher?" he queried.

The evangelist reached down into his pocket and brought out the deck of cards and the razor. He spread the cards out before him, scanning intently their red and black characters as if hoping to discover there the answer to his problem.

"Some people profess to read these things," he said. "I wish I could. I wish I had some way of knowing how I ought to feel about you, and about tonight's happenings." He eyed Sam narrowly. "How long do you expect this sort of thing to continue?" he asked.

"What sort of thing, preacher?" Sam was admitting nothing.

"Four years ago I led a revival in Memphis, Tennessee. You came there one night, the best night I ever had, as far as converts go. You came there with other cards and another razor, and twenty-three converts were taken in."

Sam could not conceal the light of admission that leaped up in his eyes. He remembered vividly, as a singer remembers a night of triumph, that evening in the tightly-packed church house in Memphis. There had been such an excess of religious fervor then that benches and chairs had been splintered as men and women, their hands tightly clenched at their sides, braced their feet against the benches in front of them and beat their backs against their own seats with quick frenzied motions like the blows of hammers. He remembered Reverend Johnson now. Seeing him now and letting his mind slip back four years, he recognized the evangelist fully, and understood now his strange outcry at the altar. The preacher had wanted to denounce him.

But the preacher was not looking at Sam now. His fingers were brushing lightly across the cards and he was talking more to himself than to the dejected, shame-stricken man in front of him.

"I remember that I asked you for the cards and the razor that night. They were sacred things for me then, with as much virtue in them as there would be in Veronica's handkerchief or in bits of the true cross. I took your story and made a fine legend out of it. It never failed to move people. It was a more wonderful thing for some of them than any story I could tell them out of the Bible. And then I learned, through some other preachers who had met up with you, what you had really been doing."

His voice now was like a piece of steel sharpened to a point and driven into the ribs. Sam wished he might grow smaller, might become something too indistinct and vaporous to be cauterised by that voice.

"I burned your cards and shattered your razor to bits," the voice mused on, the small nervous hands still dallying with the cards, "just as I ought to burn these and shatter this razor. I made a special trip back to Memphis, looked at the records of the church, and visited the people who had been converted under me. I found them good church-goers, strong in their faith. They talked to me about you, and most of them spoke of having joined church after they saw you come up to the altar. They spoke of being moved by you. I couldn't tell them that their fine steady lives, their strong religious faith, were all grounded in a lie."

Sam groaned in spirit and in truth. He wound and unwound his long legs in abject and confused misery.

"Do you know anything about Paul of Tarsus?"

"No." Sam's voice was thin and remote.

"Well," the preacher went on, "he said he was willing to be all things to convert men to Christ. Perhaps I should be willing to accept all means which contribute to their conversion. I suppose I should be willing even to accept you, without really understanding why. There are some things which we cannot understand. You and these cards, this razor, that blood money in your pocket, that fine-looking young girl waiting out there to talk to you. I cannot altogether understand why she and those eight other persons should have rejected my pleas, only to be moved by an action at whose root was the worm of deception. I should have cried out to them at the altar that they were being moved by something false, but"—he looked at Sam fiercely—"I wanted that girl up there before me down at the altar, and when I saw her coming"—his voice sank down almost to a whisper—"I forgot you and what you stood for. I only thought of my job, converting people."

He stood up as if to dismiss Sam.

"Well," he said, wearily, "I can't denounce you now, and I'm too worn out to preach to you. If I were you I'd try to mend my ways."

Sam started to the door, and then turned back.

"Are you going to tell her?"

"No. I know her kind. Fervent, intense. If I

told her, she'd hate the church and me and you. Anyway, she'll probably not see you after to-night."

Sam had a vision of her animated jet face and her straight, unyielding carriage. He turned to the evangelist.

"And if I should see a lot of her?" he asked. "I have a feeling that I'm goin' to."

"Then you must work out your own souls' salvation," the preacher said. "I wish you would go now. I'm tired; I feel defeated."

Sam suddenly felt a vast pity for this worn-out saver of souls. He wished he could do something for him. But he only walked to the door and let himself out as noiselessly as he could.

The church was soft with darkness and having shut the door behind him, he stood for a moment braced against its panels, his hands shading his eyes. At first he thought the girl might have gone, but as his sight fought through the mellowing gloom he saw her seated in one of the front pews, her face caught up in her cupped hands as if she were communing with some spirit buried deep in the inner recesses of herself.

Walking softly, he reached and touched her before she was aware of him. She started up with a quickly extinguished gasp as his fingers lay lightly on her shoulder. And then she laughed as one does when relieved of the poignancy of a needless fear.

"We could go now, miss," he said.

She rose to follow him, and it came to him that they must disturb the preacher again in order to get out, now that the front part of the church was locked and barred.

He tapped at the study door, and then opened it without waiting for a response. The minister was still seated at the table, his erratic fingers continuing their dance, his hard bright eyes burning like bits of coal. He rose as they entered, and his face assumed a petulant cast, as if they represented a recurring annoyance.

"Sorry to have to bother you again, preacher, but we can't get out no other way. All the other doors is locked."

The preacher forced himself to be polite, looking beyond Sam to the girl who stood just behind him, her face edged like a black cameo beneath the scarlet trimming of her hat.

"That's all right," he said. "This door leads right into the street. Good night and Happy New Year to you both."

"Good night, preacher, and Happy New Year." Sam turned to go, fearful lest these two have something more to say to one another than the mere good-will wishes of the New Year. "Good night, preacher. Happy New Year." The girl turned to follow Sam, but paused and caught his hands at the threshold.

"Wait for me outside, Mr. Lucas," she besought him. "I won't be long. There's something I've got to ask the preacher."

"All right, lady." He smiled at her, but he felt the pit of his stomach giving way inside him and he had a quick desire to walk away into the cold darkness and not be there when she came forth. But he turned to meet the preacher's eyes, and what he saw there reassured him.

"All right," he repeated. "I'll wait outside."

As the door swung to behind Sam, the girl went up and caught the minister's hand. Looking at her, he thought surely she was an acceptable offer on the sacrificial altar and he wished he could assume all the credit unto himself.

She was pressing his hand now and unburdening herself of a turmoil of gratitude. He heard her through the mist with which her loveliness obscured his sight.

"I never knew getting religion could be like this," she was saying. "It makes me feel like something brand new all over. I want to thank you for it. I feel like I'm going to have a good year all through, starting out this way."

He could not answer her, but he was looking at

her kindly, his usually gimlet-like eyes clouded into a gentleness by her youth and ardor.

She looked down, and her gaze resting on the table seized upon the cards lying there. They seemed the symbol of her whole life hidden there, held there, beyond any power to change, in those red and black dots. Close by, the razor was a straight edge of fire.

"If I could have those," she looked up at him impulsively, as if letting loose something she had held in check, wanting to say and yet ashamed to utter—"if I could have these to take away with me, to keep, to remember tonight by, and you, and him out there. For that's what saved me. I'd never come forward if it hadn't of been for them." She pointed to the instruments of her salvation, and she could not have hurt him more if she had taken the blade and buried it in his face. That would have been physical; this made him wince in the spirit.

He pressed her hand, and shook his head as one might at a spoiled child. "Those things are better off with me," he said, trying to laugh, but the chuckle was dry and forced. "They are the devil's own tools."

"Not now," she denied him, the light of her conviction streaming out and gathering up the light from the razor. "They are God's now. They couldn't do anybody any harm now. I want them to put away, like something holy, that I can go to and get strength from, just by looking at. Won't you give them to me?"

He thought of the pack of cards he had asked for in Memphis and of that other razor; he remembered with what reverence he had wrapped them in his handkerchief and laid them away next to his Bible, relics as vital and powerful to him then as Veronica's veil might have been or bits of the true cross. He remembered with what horror and disgust he had burned the cards afterwards and shattered the razor to bits. He could as easily tell her all that as he could take his bony fist and strike her between her two sparkling, pleading eyes.

He walked to the table, gathered up her talismans with shaking hands, unfolded his clean extra handkerchief, placed them in it, and handed the small bundle to her.

"But your handkerchief," she objected.

"Take it, please, like that," he said. "Let the handkerchief be my share in it." The bitterness in his tone was lost upon her.

She placed the small white bundle in her pocketbook.

"Good night, preacher. Happy New Year."

"Good night, sister. Happy New Year."

Chapter Three

O UTSIDE on the church steps Sam waited doggedly and defiantly. His own code of ethics never having been of a nature to induce in him an overwhelming faith in that of another, he feared, despite the promise in the minister's eyes, what might transpire back there in the study. It must be well after one o'clock, he thought, but time seemed forgotten by the happy New Year revelers who surged back and forth along the street, blowing horns, throwing colored tape, wishing one another well with happy indiscrimination. He had half a mind to join them, to let them sweep him along like a leaf caught up with other leaves in a mighty wind. What reason, what good reason, he asked himself, had he for staying here? He had done all the good he could, and if he left now he would have placed himself out of reach of doing any further harm.

"Happy New Year, Mr. Lucas. I forgot to tell you that before." He turned and saw her standing there at his side, her teeth gleaming like lights in the ebony framework of her face.

"Happy New Year, Miss Mattie," and he let his own smile go out to her without bridle or stay. He explained readily as he saw amazement and question. on her face when she heard him utter her name.

"I heard the old lady call you Mattie," he said, adding, "and I remembered it 'cause I wanted to know it. And I wouldn't mind hearin' the other part, too."

"Johnson—Mattie Johnson."

"Happy New Year, again, then, Miss Mattie Johnson." He seemed to have been made gay by her very presence, and knowing her full name became the quintessence of knowledge.

"Happy New Year, Mr. Sam Lucas," she rejoined, matching her memory against his with the pride of a child showing off a new toy.

"Which a way we goin'?" he asked.

"I live up and over, on Fifth Avenue."

They turned in the direction toward which she had pointed, and she made as if to take his arm. But she grasped only the empty sleeve of his coat. He was aware of a tremor of uneasiness running through her as she dropped the sleeve, afraid, it seemed, to anchor herself to anything of such instability. He flicked away both her embarrassment and her fears with a laugh.

"Better try the other side, ef you ain't supatitious."

"What do they say?" she queried.

"That a woman walkin' on the outside is for sale." He hoped he wasn't too forward.

"Well," she said, "I needn't mind that. I'm free, single, disengaged, and twenty-one."

"But not white." He bit his lips, wishing he might recapture these words, thinking she might be sensitive about her color.

But she only flashed her gaze on to his own dark countenance and confirmed his raillery.

"A long ways from white, but still not for sale."

Yet she crossed over and grasped his right arm, snuggled up against him, and tried to match her own mincing steps with his long, uneven strides.

They walked in silence for a few moments, as if to accustom themselves to the reality of one another, as if each were musing on the evening's happenings, and wondering for just what purposes they had been caught up and whirled about in so much space, to be set down suddenly facing one another, breathless with inquiry.

Suddenly she turned to him, her face luminous with a strange fire that smote him and made him uneasy. He had seen this same light shining on the preacher's face, but on hers it glowed with a strength that he felt might burn sheer through his masquerade and reveal him for the arrant trickster he was.

"Tell me how it felt," she said.

He wanted to ask, "What?" but he knew only too well what she meant. "You tell me," he fenced, sending up a petition to the deity of dissemblers to sustain him in this hour of imaginative need.

"Oh, it was like nothing I ever felt before," she was saying. "Like fire burning first, and then like ice, or like a knife cutting. Like fingers running up and down my back, fingers of fire and ice. It was like something pulling me out of myself, up from that bench, although my hands gripped the seat, and I told myself I wouldn't rise and go up there and bow down."

"That's how it was with me," he lied. "Like fire and ice."

He was hardly aware of what he was saying, or of her words, so avidly was he drinking in the clear beauty which seemed to drench her, spumed up and over her as she relived her new religious birth.

"I never wanted to do it that way," she went on. "I used to laugh at Aunt Mandy going to church, and shouting, clapping her hands, and running up and down the aisles, making me ashamed of her. And I only went to church with her to please her, because she wanted me to, not that I felt I needed it."

Her tone grew plaintive, as if she were chastising herself and feeling the pain of the punishment at the same time. "And now, just to think that I started out like that, making a show of myself to the people. But I couldn't help myself. When the preacher came to me, he made me mad, picking me out like that in front of all the church, as if I'd been a bad woman; and I grew stubborn, honery inside, hard like a stone, and I wouldn't go up for him or Aunt Mandy. But when you stepped up, so firm-like and decided, and threw down those cards and that razor, I felt something like fire run from the cards and the razor straight into me and burn my sins away."

He looked at her, so young and well moulded, with the marks of her childhood still lingering on her face, as if loth to be erased totally by her womanhood; and it seemed so ridiculous that she should be concerned about her sins, that he asked her, half in earnest, half in mockery:

"And did you have many sins to burn away?"

She was too far lost in her ecstasy to catch anything but the earnestness of his question. "I can't say what they were," she answered. "I suppose, whatever they were, they were all little sins. But Aunt Mattie says we all have a certain amount of sin in us, and the only way to get rid of it is by getting religion. I must have had some sin in me, else why would I have been struck like that to-night?"

"I s'pose so," he acquiesced. "But how does it make you feel now, losin' your sins?"

She looked off into space, away from him, as if she could see her sins in tangible form fading away on the horizon, distorted, impure shapes bidding her farewell forever.

"Peaceful-like," she said, "as if I could walk on air and never drop; powerful-like, as if I could walk through fire and never burn; contented-like, as if I loved everybody in the world."

"You got good religion, miss, better'n mine," he said, adroitly paving the way for future relapses. "I don't feel so sure of myself. I feel like I might stumble ag'in sometime, like I might gamble, or drink ag'in, or love too many women."

She eyed him sorrowfully, as if she had grown wise between the intaking and the releasing of a breath, and she cautioned him firmly in words she had heard at many a meeting with Aunt Mandy, and which she had unwittingly buried deep in herself for this moment's harvesting:

"You must lean hard on the Lord." And she felt as if she had uttered some pearl of wisdom which she alone had discovered and released to a weary, despondent world.

"Look," she said, suddenly, as she delved down into her pocketbook, to draw forth the preacher's handkerchief. "I'd give you these if you hadn't said what you did just then, about not being so sure of yourself. I asked the preacher for them, so I could keep them by me, to look at, to remember tonight by, and you, and him, and to get strength from when I'm weak. But they might tempt *you* away from God."

She unfolded the handkerchief, letting him gaze down on the cards and razor. In spite of his manhood, a soft film crept over his eyes and he felt as if he were seeing earth thrown upon the coffin of a dear friend. But it was not an altogether bitter potion that he was drinking; for its gall was tempered with the honey of her sentiment in wanting these things to keep; and while this liquid made him grimace, it also made him smile.

"I shall keep these always," she was saying, "in a little box, maybe in a little silver box; maybe"— this last was said defiantly, as if she set extravagance at naught where such a keepsake was concerned—"in a little golden box."

She looked at him, while the currents of their eyes mixed and ran hot and dynamic from one to the other, hers filling him with a half-regretful pride that such store should be set by his ancient, fraudulent possessions, his flowing out full and undeterred, stripped of their religious travesty, bright and heady with sensuousness, flowing over her and filling her with a vague, partly disquieting, half-happy uncertainty.

During their talking he had not noticed where she was leading him, but had turned obediently whenever the pressure on his arm had indicated a change in their course. Now she stopped suddenly before a brown-stone apartment house, an unpretentious dwelling-place for simple colored people.

"This is where I live," she said. "Thanks for seeing me home."

"Thanks for lettin' me." He stood there with nothing more to say, yet not wishing to leave.

Impulsiveness was part of her nature, as he could see by now; so he was not altogether surprised when she put her hand in his and said:

"Tomorrow is New Year's. We're having black-eyed peas and rice. Aunt Mandy has an idea it brings good luck. Won't you come and have dinner with us?"

He could have sung for happiness; instead, he was mute for joy.

"We're having turkey, too," she added, fearful lest the simple fare mentioned at first might not appeal to him.

"It wasn't that," he reassured her. "Your asking me was just so good I lost my tongue. Black-eyed peas and rice is good enough for me. What time you want me to come?"

"About eight," she said. "My name is in the bell, and you'd best take down the number of the house. You might forget it."

"I couldn't forget this house in a million years."

She gave him a smile for this extravagant speech, and went inside. He stood watching the spot where she had been for a moment, then thrust his hand into his pocket where the money, forgotten until now, made a pleasant sound. He walked over to a lamp-post where he might count the profits of his most recent conversion.

Chapter Four

A HASTY survey of his gains showed that he had over twenty dollars, enough to board and lodge him for a week at least. The minister had called it blood money, and while he had sat there in the study, cowed by the preacher's eyes and distressed by his sharp biting voice, the money had seemed tainted even to him. But now, viewed in the clearer light of his immediate needs, as the wind whipped his legs and fanged his neck and ears, this money was purified for him, as all preceding amounts similarly gained had been, by the knowledge of the good it could render his body. Though he shivered as he walked along, he was inwardly warmed by the thought of a bed at the colored Y. M. C. A., a new shirt and tie for tomorrow, and New Year's dinner with Mattie.

He slept far into the afternoon, his whole being drowned and lost in an unaccustomed sense of security. When he arose he ate frugally at the Y Cafeteria, guarding his rampant appetite in order to show a proper appreciation for Mattie's cooking. He bought a shirt colored blue like an unclouded sky, and to go with it a magenta-hued tie profusely sprinkled with yellow stars. He sat shivering behind a screen in a stuffy little tailor shop while the tailor occupied himself with his lone suit of clothes, snipping raveled ends here and there, drawing up a hole or so, fortifying buttons, and finally sponging and pressing the whole garment. Sam had never felt so beauish before, as he strutted out, his trousers still warm and damp but fronting the wind with edges sharp as razors.

She had said eight o'clock, but he was ardent and unfashionable enough to be beforehand. At seven he was standing in the vestibule of her home, grievously and painstakingly trying with the aid of a sputtering match to spell out her name in the bell. The long corridor of the ground floor, leading to the stairs, was dark and musty, and pervaded with the seeping and mingling odors of many competing New Year's dinners. Other noses more delicately nurtured might have wrinkled in rebellion; Sam's distended in joyous anticipation.

The halls were ill-lighted and labyrinthine, and he was despairing of finding the apartment when Aunt Mandy's voice shrilled down at him:

"Up this way, son."

She stood at the door of her apartment, bright and spirited, in a gay checkered dress which transformed her from the faded-looking yellow woman of the night previous into a creature sprightly and bird-like. It was as if she had worn her religious garments then, and was now attired in festive robes. There were hoops in her ears, and on her fingers glittering circles of dubious value.

"Come right on in, son," she greeted him, as if their acquaintance was founded on ages and not on hours. "I'm powerful glad you could come. The dinner'll be better with a man here instead of just us two women."

He could not answer her for a moment, searching the room for Mattie, piqued that she had not come forth to meet him instead of sending her aunt. Aunt Mandy perceived his alarm, and eased him by saying, as she led him into the small combination parlor and dining-room: "Mattie ain't got home from work yet. She'll be in about seven-thirty."

He sat down drinking in the warmth and hominess of the place, sinking comfortably into one of the huge chairs of their three-piece Michigan set, admiring the pictures in their worn, gilt frames hung at irrelevant random around the room, scenes of flowers and foods; liking in particular one study showing a fish and a rabbit stretched on a platter, the eyes of each set like glass, and their necks dripping blood. He admired the hand-made flowers stuck in ludicrous vases distributed around the room in a profusion that seemed to him the sum total of all opulence. These people made their own heat, and the small stove perched on its zinc pad gave to the room just that warmth and spirit which he felt a home should have. Here was a likable spot on which to raise his Ebenezer.

In the center of the room a table, shining with the Sunday table-cover and napery, bright like an army with banners as its much-scrubbed and polished cutlery sent forth streams of light, was set for three. The preliminary tidbits lent color and enticement to the setting; at each place was a small crêpe-paper basket filled with peanuts and white mint candy; in one dish a mass of olives with red mouths glistened; in others were radishes and celery; and through the keyhole and under the threshold slit of a door which must lead into the kitchen came the succulent odors of their dinner.

At one end of the table the cloth had been thrown back, and there, until Sam came, Aunt Mandy had been sitting, endeavoring to read her fortune with a much-used deck of cards. It seemed to Sam that the old lady was endowed with a versatile sincerity. Like Peter she was a rock, and no sturdier base could have been unearthed on which to lay the foundations of faith. She was a pillar of the church, giving of her earthly substance to a degree that was truly sacrificial, and of her time

to an extent which had made her ignorant of
nearly all else save church ritual. There was no
concert or benefit given at Mount Hebron at
which she was not present. Nothing short of being
bedridden could keep her from her Thursday-
night class and her Friday-evening prayer-meeting.
Headaches, chills, and fevers were excuses for
children, back-sliders, and sinners; a true Christian must be prepared to lap water like a dog.

Yet, though she was a rock, steadfast and im-
movable, credulous of all biblical magic, she maintained a decent and sane respect for the things of
the world, and a proper fear of the powers of darkness. She was like one caught and twined about by
two rival serpents, her religious faith straining her
in one direction, her worldly fear and inquisitive-
ness striving to draw her into an opposing channel.
Though she could shout with the best in a way
that was beautiful to behold, her light, dry body
bounding like a small playful animal endeavoring
to free itself from a cage; though she could sit perfectly still in her pew and let the Spirit gradually
steal upon her in mesmeric power until she shuddered and twitched and wrung her hands ineffec-
tually, while she uttered strange unintelligible
bird-like sounds which she was pleased to call the
gift of tongues; though she never tired of telling
at Thursday-night class and at Friday-night prayer-

meeting "how one Monday night far in the South-land my dungeon was shook and all my chains broke, and my feet was taken out of the mire and the clay and put upon the path that leads to Christ and everlasting peace"—she was not wholly removed from the world. There was much that was pagan and occult in her. Her religion was a somber coat sumptuously lined with superstition. Every nerve-center in her being tingled and responded to signs and omens. Though she was not averse to trusting serenely to the ways of Providence, she often attempted, by reading tea leaves and coffee dregs, and by consulting her cards, to speed the blessings of Heaven or to ward off, if possible, some celestial chastisement. Both sides of her nature had been touched by Mattie's conversion; she was proud to have her niece in the church; she was eager to know how her faith would stand the test, what trials might beset her, what vine-strewn pits might be dug. Last night she had knelt fervently and prayed for light and guidance in these questions; now she was endeavoring to probe Heaven's mind with her cards.

In her checkered dress, with her gold hoops swinging in her ears and her lean sulphuric fingers gleaming with their spurious jewels, she was like a gypsy who had insinuated herself in from the road with promises of revealing all futurity. Sam's fingers itched for the cards, but not for fortune-telling.

There was a romantic segment in Aunt Mandy's mind, into which she was bent to entrap and immure this long dark man. Like Pilate's wife, she was troubled in mind with vague misgivings.

Shuffling her cards, she wreathed her parchment-yellow face into a smile: "I've been tryin' to find out what the new year will bring us, son. I'd just got to this card"—she pointed to the jack of spades—"when the bell rang and up you come." She cackled with mirth at the coincidence.

Sam laughed with her, but would not leave her with her victory.

"But you knew I was comin'," he expostulated.

"No. I knew you was expected, but I didn't know you was comin' for certain. That was different."

They both laughed together at her ability to defend herself. Then he pretended to be offended at the card she had chosen to represent him.

"Don't you think this might 'a' been somebody else?" he queried, picking up the card. "Most in general I thinks of myself as the jack of *clubs*."

She scanned his ebony face carefully; then shook her head ruefully.

"Sorry, son, but the jack of spades is the best I

can do for you. Want me to tell your fortune now?"

"What would she say?" he asked, thinking of the earnestness of her voice last night and of the unstinted fervor with which Mattie had entered upon her new life.

"What she don't know won't hurt her." Aunt Mandy riffled the cards vigorously, and set herself to scan the future and to endeavor, if possible, to shape some of its happenings to her own liking.

She plumped them down before him.

"Cut," she commanded. "Three times toward yourself."

He drew his chair up to the table and did as she bade. She turned the three stacks over, and the sight of the well-loved black and red dots set him tingling with desire and regret.

The old lady's fingers caught on to one of the stacks like greedy talons, and Sam, watching her, knew that in her way and for her purposes she was as devoted to these painted oblong bits of cardboard as he.

She spread the first stack out fan-shaped in her hand, and then laid it down. Then she took up the second pack, which she considered more carefully, for it held the jack of spades.

"That's you," she said, showing it to him again as if he had never seen it before. She studied the cards intently, then looked up at him, her eyes charged with mystery and malice.

"You've been a rounder in your time," she accused him—"a rounder and a bad man. There ain't much that's bad that you haven't done; you've drunk, and you've cussed, and you've took the Lord's name in vain. And you've fit. Look at that scar on your cheek!"

So sudden was this accusation, and so naïve, that he was totally disconcerted. He raised his hand to his cheek and felt the smooth ashen line as if it were something unfamiliar.

"But all that's over now," she went on, her claws spreading and tapping the cards. "All that's over; now you've got God in your heart and you're going to settle down and be a different man. A woman's coming into your life."

"A woman?" Sam was eager now. "What she look like?"

"She's thin and dark and good. And she likes you."

Thin and dark and good, he thought; and sometimes she wears a red-and-black hat, he hoped.

"How you know she likes me?"

She looked up at him, all the malice gone now, only the mystery prevailing.

"Cards don't lie," she said.

"But don't you think cards is evil?" Sam

wanted to know, finding it strange that such a good churchwoman could fondle them so lovingly.

"It all depends on the kind of cards you have and what you do with them." Aunt Mandy leaned across the table in a philosophic and instructive attitude, seriously ready to produce extenuations for one side of her nature, and to demonstrate that it in no wise interfered with the other. "Them cards you had last night was evil, before you threw them down there at the mo'ner's bench, but when you threw them down, all the sin went out of them, just like Christ sent the evil spirits out of some man or other, and drove them into the pigs. You remember?"

"No, I disremember that story," he answered, truthfully, repressing a desire to simulate wisdom, for fear the avowal of so much information might lead to technical questioning.

"Well, anyhow, the devils left the man, just like the evil left them cards, and now they ain't nothing but goodness in them. As for my cards, they ain't evil, 'cause I uses them for good. If I gambled with them, then that would be sin. I only use them to find out how to keep out of the devil's way. And they've hoped me out a heap of times."

There was the click of a key, and from where he sat looking down the small hall, Sam saw Mattie enter. Aunt Mandy whisked the cards from the table and out of sight.

Mattie was dressed as she had been the preceding evening; with her eyes lively with expectation and apology, she seemed to have grown more attractive with the passing of a day. The severe cold had nipped her face until her cheeks, dark as they were, were centered with a soft struggling purple. She made no attempt to conceal the genuine pleasure which she felt in seeing him again; and he rose up, long and awkward, and thrilled at the simple sight of her.

"I'm so glad you could come," she said. "And I'm sorry to be late, but Mrs. Brandon had people in to dinner today, and I always have to serve when she gives a high-toned dinner. But she's awfully nice, just the same. I guess you've heard of her."

"No, I don't know no white folks here," Sam answered, rejecting the honor.

"But she's not white. She's colored. Dr. Brandon's wife. They're very rich." She was ashamed of his ignorance.

"Oh, you work for colored people." He said it as if he were simply acknowledging a bit of information, but she felt that she had lost caste with him.

While they were talking, Aunt Mandy had been

busy carrying in platter after platter of steaming, odorous food. Mattie and her aunt managed to strike the middle way between two extremes of colored people. They neither pampered the belly while the back went bare, nor perished in fine clothes.

Today Aunt Mandy had attempted hopefully to prepare a meal which would be prophetic of the year's abundance. There were black-eyed peas and rice; these were for luck. But for the special glory of New-Year's day there were turkey and peas, potatoes of both kinds, one dish of them mashed, rising up white and frothy, the other dish heaped with large yams that had burst their covering and were now bleeding sweetness through their wounds. There were collard greens, verdantly rich like spinach, but infinitely better tasting; biscuits; and pies of sweet potatoes and mincemeat.

They ate for the most part in silence, finding the business of eating too heavenly to be defiled by many words. Only with their eyes meeting and holding above their plates, with their fingers brushing as a platter was passed, and through that infinite understanding which man has with woman and which surpasses all other brands of wisdom, did Mattie and Sam speak to one another and respond.

Sam had hoped there might be something to drink, some home-made wine at least, perhaps something more potent. But there was only coffee, served along with the meal. Aunt Mandy couldn't abide the smell of liquor, and Mattie didn't like it.

After dinner Aunt Mandy pleaded fatigue and a headache, feeling free to pamper herself since there was no church meeting scheduled for that evening, and went into her room to lie down.

"I'll do the dishes," Mattie called after her.

"I wish I could help you," Sam said, looking ruefully at his left sleeve, "but I can't do anything along that line."

"Well, you can come out in the kitchen and sit with me while I wash them."

He helped her clear the table, making trip after trip from the dining-room into the kitchen, carrying a single dish or a fistful of knives and forks in his one strong hand. Once or twice they collided, and turned to laugh at one another. She thought he was decidedly handsome; he thought she was pretty, but different from the usual run of women he had known.

He drew a chair up to the kitchen sink, close beside her, where he could watch the movements of her dark hands, darting in and out of the hot, soapy water like small black fish. She chattered as she worked, telling him all about herself. He sat there with greased insides, a little heavy and a trifle sleepy, but happy to hear her voice beating on his ears. Between the washing and the drying of the dishes she told him all there was to tell. She was twenty-two. She had been born in Alabama. There had been no brothers or sisters. When she was seven her mother had died, and her father had sent her up to New York to live with his brother and Aunt Mandy, because they had no children and wanted her, and because her father had been frightened at finding himself left alone with a seven-year-old girl. Uncle Benjamin and Aunt Mandy had sent her to school and life had been rosy. At first her father had sent small sums of money from time to time to pay for her keep. But after a while these ceased, and even his letters. Though they had written to friends back in her home town, all they could learn was that her father had left, bound no one knew where. They had never heard from him since. But Aunt Mandy and Uncle Ben hadn't minded, because they loved her. They had kept her in school and had even placed her in high school, where she had begun to study French and a terrible kind of arithmetic called algebra.

Sam's eyes were shining with admiration.

"Say somethin' in French," he begged.

"Oh, I didn't take much," she excused herself "and I've forgotten that." And then she went on. While she was in her second year in high school Uncle Ben had died.

"And colored people don't leave any money, you know," she wound up. "So I had to quit school and go to work to help Aunt Mandy; and I've been working ever since."

"Tell me where to put these." He held a stack of dishes in his hand, balancing them nicely.

"Just over there in the closet, any place. I can put them in order later on. I've been working for Mrs. Brandon for five years now."

"You say she's colored?" Again she felt the displeasure in his voice and it riled her.

"Yes. I like working for my own. You don't like working for them?"

" 'Tain't that I don't like workin' for them, 'cause I never did work for them, but I hear they ain't so easy to get along with; too uppity."

"That's not so," she was wringing the dishtowel more vigorously than was her wont. "Black folks know better how to treat black folks every time."

"Well, let's don't fuss." He turned his eyes on her, and she thought they were the finest she had ever seen.

The dishes were all clean now and had been

put away. Back in the parlor they sat facing one another, between them the small glowing stove. Outside they could hear the horns and sirens and all the strange confused noises of people walking the streets in search of pleasure.

"You're like all the women," he accused her. "You've left out the part I wanted to hear."

"What part?"

"About your fellers."

"Oh, them? I used to have fellers when I was in high school, and even before; every girl had a beau, but since I started working I been too busy to think about fellers."

"Every woman needs a man." He made her drop her eyes before him.

"Tell me about you," she asked.

A braggart at heart and a weaver of fanciful tales, he wanted nothing better.

"Let's start at the jumping-off place." He stretched his legs and arched his head back to make himself comfortable. "I was born in Texas in a little town so small I don't need to tell its name, 'cause nobody would know it. 'Tain't on the map. Ma had a child every year, and paw was crazy tryin' to get enough to feed them, but they kept on comin'. I didn't have no schoolin'. I can read my name if it's writ big enough, but if you writ it small I wouldn't know it. There was ten of us when I left home over ten years ago, when I was eighteen. God knows how many there is now. Since then I've seen a heap of towns and places. I always liked travelin'. I'm what they call a travelin' man. I had my arm cut off by a train when I was stealin' a ride. Now I'm here in New York and I think it's so fine, and I think you're so nice, I wish my travelin' days was over. That's all about me."

But it wasn't all; it was simply all he willed to tell her. He could have told her of his meeting over eight years ago with the huge blue-gummed man who had taught him the material value of religion. He had forgotten the man's name but he would always be grateful to him.

"My people will do anything when they're happy," the man had said, providing conversation for a group of street-corner stragglers. "I bet if some one went in and threw down a pack of cards and said he had religion the whole church would board and lodge him."

Sam had listened silently, but at the next town he came to he had tried it, as a novice, without even searching out a revival meeting; he had tried it at a simple prayer-meeting service and had been feasted and fattened for days before he shook the dust of his first conversion from the soles of his feet and went on his heathen way. At first he had used the cards alone; later the idea of the razor had come to him; a heavenly vision he called it; and the maneuver had proved a tremendous and ever-mounting success. After he lost his arm, his conversions came upon him more often.

And they were far more profitable; for the sight of his armless sleeve always tinged the religious fervor of his victims with pity, making them give him money. These things he could not tell her.

"How did you get that scar?" she asked him.

"I got that a long time ago. A man was beatin' his wife and I hit him. He cut me."

He could have added that the quarrel between his adversary and his wife had pivoted around himself, but he did not care to tell her this.

He was beginning to like her and to desire her. Had she been another woman, he would have had her in his arms by now, or would have been on his way, rebuffed but merry. He had had few rebuffs, in most cases far more encouragement than he was receiving now.

"I've bought a new dress for Sunday," she was saying, rousing him up out of his thoughts, which had begun to be lecherous. "Couldn't we go together?"

"Where?" The finer edges of his mind hadn't been given enough warning, and they failed to function at this abrupt invitation.

"Why, to church! The minister is going to take all the new converts in together." There was genuine chagrin on her face that he should have forgotten something so important.

"Sure," he promised. "I'll come by for you." He hadn't intended to go back. He had hoped to lose himself in the life of the city until he should feel an itching in his feet to be gone to a new habitat and new spiritual conquests. But to sit beside her in her new dress, himself wearing his new shirt and tie, here was a pleasure worth any heresy he might commit.

Chapter Five

WHEN Sam and Mattie and Aunt Mandy entered the church on Sunday morning, their appearance was greeted with a low murmur of excited recognition, more for Aunt Mandy who was one of the veteran worshipers, and for Sam, whose dramatic conversion from sin had already become a story to swear by, than for Mattie. Aunt Mandy was subdued in both mind and body, accoutered physically and spiritually in a manner best befitting the Lord's day. The most celebrated teller of fortunes in the world could not have caught her ear this morning, nor could the glossiest, newest deck of cards have intrigued her hands. She was dressed entirely in black; her diminutive foreign-yellow face was serene beneath her small black hat and totally unreflective of the world's wrongs. Gone were the gold hoops from her ears, and the flashy mendacious jewels from her fingers. This being the first Sunday in the month, it was also Communion day, and she was not one to reach out for the sacred wafer and wine with hands polluted by jewelry. Mattie, too, was soberly dressed, a bit of her dark-blue dress showing beneath her black coat. But Sam was colorful in his blue shirt and his radiant tie sprinkled with yellow stars.

This was the evangelist's last day; the evening sermon would be his last before he should be on to another city, carrying in his slight dynamic body his thunderbolts of wrath against all that was carnal and sinful. He seemed tired this morning, and to spare himself, as if he felt that no wild rallying at this last moment could save those who had not heeded his entreaties throughout the week. As his Scripture lesson he read from the twenty-first chapter of Revelations, from the twenty-first through the twenty-fifth verse:

"And the twelve gates were twelve pearls: every several gate was one of pearl: and the street of the city was pure gold, as it were transparent glass.

"And I saw no temple therein: for the Lord God Almighty and the Lamb are the temple of it.

"And the city had no need of the sun, neither of the moon, to shine in it: for the glory of God did lighten it, and the lamb is the light thereof.

"And the nations of them which are saved shall walk in the light of it: and the kings of the earth do bring their glory and honor into it.

"And the gates of it shall not be shut at all by day: for there shall be no night there.

. . . "For there shall be no night there."

Such was his text. Quietly and reverently he developed it, laying aside his abundant store of vitriol and denunciation. He wished to leave with them a feeling of security and promise. He was curiously tranquil as he talked to them, seeming by some colossal willfulness to check the usual excited gestures of his hands and feet. He was telling them of heaven, and the vast audience was like putty in his hands as they listened to him. Whatever doubts and fears they might have later, when they should file out into the cold of a real world where all was surely not as they would have fashioned it, nor as a God of infinite compassion would have done, they were wandering now in the golden streets of illusion. Their many-colored hands were caressing smooth walls of jasper, and wherever they turned rich streams of milk and honey flowed. There were four and twenty elders bowing down in shining robes and glittering crowns before an indefinable being of unfathomable benignity who was God. And close beside, shining like the sun, and healed forever of the nailprints in his hands and feet, and with his flowing side forever stanched, was Christ, their brother.

Reverend Johnson's voice was so quiet and unpretentious that no one shouted. There was no active demonstration beyond the voicing of a few low-breathed hallelujahs and amens, and the soft dabbing here and there at eyes that could not remain dry envisioning so much peace. Sam felt mean and ashamed, but it was all a well-told fairy tale for him, and he could not, no matter how desperately he tried, feel conviction. Beside him Mattie sat tense and beautiful, her face erased of every doubt that might have lingered there, her whole being given over in unrestrained credulity to the glories of the heavenly landscape. She wished the preacher might go on and on describing these scenes of a life in which she now felt that she had a part, for was she not now a co-heir with Christ and all the saved of the world?

"And there shall be no night there," the minister was closing; his voice floated soft and low with enticement and promise, "no night, but every day shall shine brighter than the brightest sun this world has ever seen. And all that light shall come from God's own face, and light up the whole heavens, and we that have been purified and washed in Jesus' blood shall walk forever and forever in that light."

Amen. He sat down as if thoroughly outworn, less from physical exertion than from spiritual exhaustion. The church, awakened from its transport, droned like one large fly.

But only for a moment. Reverend Drummond,

the pastor of the church, arose to extend the invitation. He spoke in deep, guttural tones, which seemed to come from the farthest abyss of the stomach:

"We have listened to and enjoyed Reverend Johnson's beautiful sermon, and we know what joys are laid up for us in the kingdom of God. Now we want to welcome into our midst those brothers and sisters who gave themselves to Christ during the week. We want them to become full members of the church now, before Reverend Johnson leaves us, so he can see what good work he has done for the Master. While the choir sings, I want our new members to come forward and stand here in front of the altar. And any, even now, who want to come with them, may do so. There are no set times with Christ. He is always ready to receive."

The organ groaned softly, while the choir, a mingling of light and dark faces in white robes, began to sing:

"I'm so glad I got my religion in time,
I'm so glad I got my religion in time,
O my Lord, O my Lord, what shall I do?"

For a moment it seemed as if the new converts had reconsidered; no one stirred. The minister stood waiting; the evangelist had risen and stood beside him, ready to welcome in the fruits of his own endeavors. Finally a man came forward, and seemed to give the signal which less valiant converts had awaited. People began to come forward from all parts of the church. Mattie nudged Sam.

"Shall we go up now?" she asked.

"Yes," he said so low that she divined his response by the nod of his head rather than by the sound of his voice. It was all right for him to go up and sham by himself, but he felt like a criminal going up with her, trailing his insincerity in the wake of her pure, exalted faith.

He followed her up the aisle, and they stood there together, two such delightful specimens of handsome blackness that the kindly feelings of the audience went out to them in great waves of sympathy and pride.

They stood there, warm and self-conscious, two out of thirty-eight others turning their backs on the things of the world and starting on the path called straight and narrow. They found that joining church was more than the mere giving of their names. The officers and leading members of the church, somber men and women, filed by, shaking their hands and wishing them well. The two ministers came down and welcomed them into the church. The evangelist had reached Sam and had extended his hand without recognizing him. As he looked into Sam's face he seemed to stiffen, but only for a moment. He wrung his hand heartily and spoke to him.

"May you be a good soldier in the army of the Lord, my brother."

And to Mattie, "May the blood of Christ keep you forever in His way."

The church clerk came forward to take their names and addresses.

Reverend Drummond had been keeping pace with the clerk as he went from convert to convert, stopping to speak softly and earnestly to each of them for a few moments, after which he would call forth a name, in answer to which some member of the church would come forward to shake the convert's hand. Sam's spiritual trafficking had been large enough and frequent enough for him to realize what these actions portended. The converts were being assigned to their week-night classes. He wondered what night Mattie would choose; whatever her choice, it would also be his. This would not be his first enrollment which had not terminated in attendance.

Before the minister reached them, Aunt Mandy, happy and proud of the occasion, floated down the aisle like a large-sized doll. She kissed Mattie as she had seen so many other women do, while she envied them, when their daughters or friends joined church; she even gave Sam a swift embarrassing peck on the cheek. And then she whispered to Mattie:

"You must join the Thursday-night class. That's my class, and our leader, Brother Green, is the best of them all. He's got more grace than all the rest put together. And he can pray like ——" Words failed her and she simply spread her hands out as if unable to describe the colossal powers of petition resident in her leader.

The minister stood beside them. Sam heard him say, as if he were declaiming by rote something ingrained into him and like food become part of him through much repetition: "The Methodist Church offers its members weekly spiritual sustenance through its class-meetings and Friday-night prayer-meetings. Which class will you join, sister, Monday, Tuesday, Wednesday, or Thursday night?"

Mattie chose Thursday night. She looked anxiously at Sam when the question was put to him; pleasure mounted her eyes when he chose the same night.

"Brother Green," called Reverend Drummond, turning from them to summon a short black man with small red eyes and a large mouth topped and flanked by a bristly mustache.

"I give these new converts over to you, Brother

Green," he said, "Look after them the way you do the rest of your members, and don't let the devil lay hold on them again."

Back in his seat again, squeezed tightly and pleasantly against Mattie, his flesh throbbing warmly beneath this remote and artificial contact, Sam felt that he had gone through his ordeal like a man, and that no more would be demanded of him now. But he reckoned without Mattie and the ways of the African Methodist Episcopal Church. For a while he sat in peace, narrowing his gaze into a sidelong slit that shut out all else from his sight and only revealed to him, clean and undisturbed, like a small black cameo cut out of space, Mattie's serene black features. Truly, he told himself, she was lovely and to be desired, so lovely and straight, with the spirit of contemplation and religious zeal easing her face of all else save of thinking on God, her beauty able to shine out beyond the darkness of her costume. He trembled to think how glorious she would look in a dress of flaming red, with bright beads around her throat, rings upon her fingers, metal bands dangling and jingling from her wrists, and she herself caught and whirled about in the mazes of a dance. The picture was rapturous and he closed his eyes, shutting out the real Mattie, filling the dark behind his lids with the gayer Mattie of his imagination. And whirling and twirling her was a jaunty black fellow whose eyes were deep electric currents and whose one arm was as good as two.

Then into his dream of music and fleshly joy there beat the consciousness of that flesh which the church has made her own, and which she sacrifices month after month in prayer and consecration. The white cloth on the table in front of the pulpit had been removed; and there cut in minute cubes in small silver dishes was the bread symbolizing the body of Christ, and in small liqueur glasses was the wine which was his blood.

The evangelist was speaking, and Sam writhed like a rat caught in a trap as he realized what was being said: "Our Lord says the last shall be first and the first last in His kingdom; therefore I have asked Reverend Drummond to let the converts commune at the first table, even before the officers of the church, that we may do our share in fulfilling what has been written. Will the converts come and kneel here before me to eat of that food which is not of the world?"

Sam tasted the gorge of horror and remorse rising in his throat to sicken him. He had no faith; that he was a cheat and a beat he had already acknowledged to himself many times over, but more in praise of his cleverness than in disparagement of his morals. But this he could not, would not do, partake of Communion. The white altar, the cubes of bread, the wine, these were all church magic, powerful ritual with which his scorn and unbelief might not cope. He would not go up, not even for Mattie. But already she had touched him, and quicker than they had spurted up in him had sent his rebellious thoughts draining out of him. He followed her to the altar and knelt down beside her, straining himself against her as if to melt his own unworthiness into her perfect faith.

"Wherefore ye that do truly and earnestly repent of your sins, and are in love and charity with your neighbors, and intend to lead a new life, following the commandments of God, and walking from henceforth in his holy ways, draw near with faith, and take this holy Sacrament to your comfort; and, devoutly kneeling, make your humble confession to Almighty God."

Sam leaned across the rail, trying hard to reconcile himself to his surroundings. He *was* in love and charity with his neighbors; for he didn't care enough about other people to wish them ill, and he *was* in love. But not with God. With Mattie. It was not for God's bread and wine that he was here. It was for the bread and wine that she could give him.

"Almighty God, unto whom all hearts are open,

*all desires known, and from whom no secrets are
hid, cleanse the thoughts of our hearts by the in-
spiration of Thy Holy Spirit, that we may perfectly love Thee, and worthily magnify Thy holy
name, through Jesus Christ our Lord. Amen."*

The minister's voice was a denunciation in his
ears. Perhaps it was true, that all his desires and
thoughts and meannesses were known to God,
that some great eye was shining down angry and
baleful, its unseen rays probing the very depths
of his thoughts, ferreting out the deep unclean
recesses of his heart. What awful hurt lay hid for
him in those pellets of bread? Would they strangle
him as he swallowed them in his unbelief and
deceit? Would the beaded red wine, so beneficial
to these that believed and drank it in faith, burn
like viper's venom for him, and leave him lying
there at the altar, writhing in agony as a testament
of the wrath of Heaven? He wanted to rise and
flee. But he could not before so many people, and
in her sight. He closed his eyes and yearned desperately toward belief and faith; but his heart was
cold and responseless.

*"The body of our Lord Jesus Christ, which was
given for thee, preserve thy soul unto everlasting
life. Take and eat this in remembrance that Christ
died for thee; and feed on Him in thy heart by
faith, with thanksgiving."*

He looked up and saw the Reverend Drummond standing before him offering him the cubes of bread; behind him was the evangelist, bearing the wine. Sam's hand lay rigid at his side as his dark frightened face mirrored plainly the great struggle transpiring there. The evangelist leaned over and spoke to him, a direct message from one man to another, "Take and eat it, my brother; it was given for such as you."

Sam reached out, took one of the pellets and swallowed it. It went down easily; it tasted the same as any other bread. Assurance flooded him.

"The blood of our Lord Jesus Christ, which was shed for thee, preserve thy soul and body unto everlasting life. Drink this in remembrance that Christ's blood was shed for thee, and be thankful."

"Drink, brother; this is the blood of Christ that washes us white as snow."

The evangelist was smiling at him as if he understood his doubts and distress. The penetrating brown eyes were soft and gentle, filmed over by the beauty of the service. Sam took and drank, and as the tiny sip of liquid slid harmlessly down his throat all his fears vanished and his former arrogance and scorn sprouted up with renewed vigor. Far from being poison, it was not even wine that they served, but a mild grape-juice. He raised his head and looked down the long line of communicants. Their hands were spread out across the white altar-covering like so many flags of supplication and truce; their heads were submissive, their faces, of all colors, were tense and strained; all their being seemed surrendered to some divine force. At the far end of the altar a woman had suddenly gone limp; she lay stretched across the rail, her hands hanging motionless before her, short cries that might have been of pleasure or of pain issuing from her sagging mouth. At Sam's side Mattie knelt with her face hid in her hands.

"The love of God be with you all. Arise and go in peace." The evangelist was sending them away with his blessing. Sam and Mattie rose together, and he saw that her face was glowing and that down her cheeks tears flowed free and unrestrained.

When the services were over Aunt Mandy informed them that, as was her custom, she gave the Lord's day entirely over to His praise and service; therefore she was not going home for dinner, but would have her dinner in the church dining-room, and then would stay for the adult Bible class, for the young people's meeting in the afternoon, and so be ready and on hand for the evening service. Mattie said she would not remain, but would go home, and return for the evening service. Sam offered to see her home.

They walked along in a silence which was mainly fear of themselves, fear of the fierce desires at the roots of their beings that were drawing them nearer and nearer to one another. Sam had forgotten the services of the church as soon and as lightly as he had stepped across its threshold out into the sharp January sun. All that he was concerned with now was the woman at his side, an unquestionably attractive woman into whose life he had come without thought or warning. She was pressed close against him, and it seemed to him that, despite the cold, her hand on his sleeve had scorched through the fabric and was burning the naked blackness of his skin. He wished he knew how to tackle her; for he felt that she was like some new and strange being, unlike the other women he had known. Those others had been like himself, creatures of action and not of speech. They had been bold and rampant, and the few words they uttered had always found in him a masterly interpreter. He knew when a flippant word meant "Take me," and when it meant "Leave me be." But this girl with the small red mouth that he would like to lean over and invade, with the slight hard body that he yearned to crush, expending on it all the concentrated vigor of his lone arm, was strange and mysterious. She seemed near at hand, as close as if they were linked together by a strip of flesh, yet inaccessible, as if getting religion and joining church had suddenly grown walls about her and shut her away from the world. Her eyes smiled at him, but their message was neither "Take me" nor "Leave me be," but rather their unspoken word was "Speak to me" and "Tell me things." The palm of his hand was moist with panic.

As for Mattie, her suffering and doubts were as acute as his. Her mind was as alive as a beehive with questions for which she could find no ready answer. Into the clear stream of her newly-found happiness in her religion, this man's long, lean body was striding, rippling the calm surface of the water, churning up widening whirlpools of passion. She knew that he and the church were now ineradicable parts of her, and she clutched his arm fiercely for fear that he might fade out of her life as quickly and as unexpectedly as he had come. Why had they met? Why had she hardened her heart against the evangelist, and leashed her tongue to silence in scorn of him and his entreaties, only to run like water to the altar at the sight of this man and his cards and his razor? Why at his side did she feel peace and ease and comfort, a security deep and plentiful like falling into a downy bed and sleeping care and thought away? She had pity for him; she could feel the pity welling up in her at the thought of his arm long ago rotted away and gone to earth while he still walked; she felt pity and love surge through her as she looked up at the ashen scar on his cheek; she wanted to brush it with her lips and hair. She thought of the cards and the razor hid away at home in the evangelist's handkerchief; her mind slipped back to her first Communion, so short a while ago, with Sam there at her side, pressed against her, giving her greater peace and imbuing the bread and the wine with a larger significance. She would like to keep this man at her side always. Suddenly she shuddered at the thought that he might leave, and the palm of her hand oozed desperate sweat, moistening his coat.

They were near her home now and she must find some way to keep him with her. She chose the simplest.

"You must come in and have dinner with me. I'll be lonely with Aunt Mandy not here, and I hate eating alone."

She felt silly as she asked him, but the strategem was welcome to him and saved him from taking the initiative.

Upstairs, after she had changed her dress for a stiff white kitchen frock, she let him follow her

into the kitchen and take his place beside her at
the sink. He stalked the quick movements of her
fingers as she pared the potatoes or opened a can.
He was humiliated that he could not do this last
for her. She laughed at him, and told him to try
his lone hand at making coffee.

After dinner, as they sat before the fire, so
brooding a trouble lay on his face that she was
troubled too, and wondered if he were slipping
away in his thoughts, though there beside her.

"A penny for your thoughts," she bantered
him.

"They's worth more'n a penny, 'cause I was
thinkin' of you." He turned to her with such
whole-hearted admiration shining in his eyes that
she blessed her dark skin which hid from him the
hot flush of embarrassment and pleasure which
leaped to her cheeks.

"What were you thinking?"

"I was thinkin' how a woman needs a man."
His voice broke in a frightened quaver. He had
never had to talk to women before and he was
finding it worse than physical hurt.

"A man needs a woman as well as a woman
needs him." She wanted to lead him on to say
what she yearned for, and yet she did not care to
seem the aggressor.

"I think you're mighty pretty; I ain't never seen

a woman prettier." He leaned over and took her hand. She let him have it easily, and he hid it in his own.

"It's mighty little," he said.

"Yes," she assented.

"If I was well and good and had a job, I could be bold and ask you to tie up with me, and even be hopin' you'd do it." His voice was distant and renunciatory, and she felt he might be slipping away.

"But you *are* good," she gainsaid him, hoping he might read in her contradiction her desire that he also be brave. "Christ's blood has washed you free of sin. And you are well and strong."

He passed over her ignorance of his spiritual health; this was one point on which he would never openly enlighten her. But he thought of his arm and feared that she was being charitable and pitying to spare him hurt.

"Oh, I'm well enough," he confessed, "but a one-armed man can't find much to do."

"Where there's a will there's a way." Her whole-souled love and affection took up this poor platitude and arrayed it in golden threads of wisdom. "Mrs. Brandon could find you something to do, maybe something there at her house with me. If not, something some place else; she knows everybody in Harlem. She would help you if I asked her."

She had spoken breathlessly, as if to ward off an interruption.

"And you would ask her for me?"

"Gladly." He caught the love in her voice, as if it had been a ball that she had tossed to him.

He thought of the women he had known before, dark and fair, small and large; they had come to him easily like water thrown upon a hill that has no other way to run but down; and like water he had run from them when he had tired. But these women had been different; they had been his kind, and when he had told them of his professional religion, they had laughed hard, throwing their heads back and showing their teeth, and they had called him damned tricky, and had said that the joke was all on God and that it was a good one. But Mattie had taken his cards and his razor and wrapped them up in a handkerchief, and had put them away, as something to keep her strong. She was not one to be taken and left; she would want a preacher, witnesses, a license to be framed, and a true husband.

He could read his doom in her face: no conquest for a fitful expenditure of passion, but love that was deep and severe like a halter around his neck. He sat with half-closed eyes weighing the good and evil of it. The evil of it: no more wandering off at will, begging a ride, coming into a strange town, letting his eyes burn into and melt some strange attractive woman's resistance; no more striding down a church aisle clutching in his hand a greasy deck of cards and a sharp polished razor, feeling in himself a power deeper than the preacher's. The good of it: this woman whose very existence now had for its corner stone his own untrustworthy self; an entrance into the comfort and peace of this home, deep chairs, and a fire in a shining stove; a job; children, perhaps.

Her hand lay limp upon her lap where she had let it fall when he had released it. He leaned over and took it again, decision in his pressure.

"Then, Miss Mattie, could you marry me?"

"I couldn't marry no other man."

So simple a statement, so baldly said, in a low, hushed voice that was ashamed of its avowal, but it was more important to them than the rising and falling of kingdoms, than revolutions in China and Russia, than lynchings in Alabama, than a fire in the house might have been, or a murder in the next apartment.

He was no longer shy of her now; all his manhood and assertiveness returned. He rose and took her by the hand and led her to the sofa, where they might sit together. They sat there, taut and strained, his arm hard around her, as if the sinews and bone of it realized that they were doing a double duty.

Chapter Six

CONSTANCIA BRANDON, for whom Mattie worked, was the mirror in which most of social Harlem delighted to gaze and see itself. She was beautiful, possessed money enough to be willful, capricious, and rude whenever she desired to deviate from her usual suave kindness; and she was not totally deficient in brains. Tall and willowy, with a fine ivory face whose emaciation spelled weakness and weariness, she quickly dispelled such false first impressions when she began to talk, with either her eyes or her tongue, in the use of both of which she was uncommonly gifted. Her gray eyes had strange contractile powers, narrowing into the minutest slits of disbelief and boredom, or widening into incredibly lovely globes of interest and amazement. They were not the windows of her soul, but they were the barometers by which one might gauge her interest in what he was saying.

Synthesis seemed to have had no part in her making. She had been born in Boston, and baptized Constance in the Baptist Church; but at

sixteen she had informed her astounded parents
and her equally astounded and amused friends
that thenceforth her name was to be Constancia;
that she found the religious ecstasies of the Baptist
and Methodist faiths too harrowing for her nerves;
and that she would attempt to scale the heavenly
ramparts by way of the less rugged paths of the
Episcopalian persuasion. From the beginning her
manner was grand, and she gave one the impression that the great triumvirate, composed of God,
the Cabots, and the Lodges, had with her advent
into the world let down the color bar and been
reorganized, to include hereafter on an equal
footing Constancia Brown. She had never experienced any racial disturbances or misgivings, at-
tributing her equanimity on this score to one
English grandfather, one grandfather black as
soot, one grandmother the color of coffee and
cream in their most felicitous combination, one
creole grandmother, and two sane parents. She
was interested in her geneology only because she
wanted to ascertain if there really were somewhere
in the medley a gypsy woman or man whose slowly
diminishing blood was responsible for her inces-
sant and overwhelming love of jewelry. From the
moment her ears had been pierced they had never
been devoid of ornaments; sleeping or waking,

she gave evidence of wise and charming invest-
ments in bracelets, rings, and pendants.

But her tongue was her chief attraction, orna-
ment, and deterrent. Her linguistic powers, aided
by an uncanny mnemonic ability, had brought her
high honors at Radcliffe and the headlong devotion of George Brandon. Her schoolmates called
her Lady Macbeth, not that she was tragic, but
that she never spoke in a monosyllable where she
could use a longer word; she never said "buy"
when she might use "purchase," and purchased
nothing to which she might "subscribe." The first
night he met her at an Alpha Phi Alpha fraternity
ball George Brandon had pleased her mightily by
dubbing her Mrs. Shakespeare.

George Brandon, short, thick-set, light brown,
and methodical, was an Oklahoma Brandon whose
very finger tips were supposed to smell of oil and
money. Constancia, whose lawyer father enjoyed
a comfortable if not opulent living, had really
lacked for no good thing, and so had been able
to meet George Brandon with a disinterestedness
and reserve that other young girls of colored Boston had not been able to simulate. She had been
amused at his enervated, drawling speech and his
dog-like devotion to her, but from that first meeting she had harbored kindly feelings for him because he had recognized her verbal literary ability

by the sobriquet of Mrs. Shakespeare. It was inevitable, then, that after six months of frantic courting she should have accepted him when he pleaded that if she failed to do so he would be in no fit condition to be graduated from the Harvard Medical College.

"Not for your money, my dear," she had assured him, "nor for any inherent and invisible pulchritude in yourself, but in order to spare to the world an accomplished physician, will I enter the enchanted realms of wedlock with you."

George had been happy to have her, even on the basis of so stilted and unromantic an acceptance. But the small-sized Oklahoma town to which he had taken her had not been able to reconcile itself to Mrs. Shakespeare. The small group of the Negro *élite* found her insufferable; they never knew what she was talking about. When she was hostess her guests generally left feeling that they had been insulted by her grandiose manners and complicated words; when she was guest her hostess never knew whether her comments on the party were commendable or derogatory. Matters fared no better at the monthly interracial meetings where the races met to exchange ideas and mutual good-will pledges, but not to touch hands. Constancia was elected secretary of the association, and thereafter the minutes were totally unintelligible save to herself, and when read made the bewildered workers for racial adjustment feel guilty of dark and immoral intentions. Mrs. Marshall, the wife of the white Baptist minister, and Mrs. Connelly, the wife of the leading white merchant, resented beyond concealment Constancia's chic vestments, blazing rings, and pendants; nor did they like the composed tone in which she would rise to say, "I unequivocally disagree with Mrs. Marshall," or, "I feel that Mrs. Connelly is in grievous error on this question."

In Oklahoma the Brandons could keep no servants; for Constancia had a strong democratic leaning which would not permit her to speak down to her menials. "I shall speak as I always do," she would say to the vainly expostulating George, "and they must learn to understand me. I do not want to embarrass them by making them self-conscious, by causing them to think that I do not believe that they have as much intelligence as I." And she continued to exhort her unintelligent help to "Come hither," to "Convey this communication to the doctor," or to "Dispatch this missive," until in utter self-defense they rebelled, and in true native fashion quit without giving notice.

Finally, at the repeated prayers of their respective ladies, the Reverend Mr. Marshall and Mr. Connelly, along with several colored members of the interracial committee, intimated to George that for the sake of racial amity it would be better if Constancia no longer kept the minutes of the meetings. And it was in order to placate Constancia for this loss of power and prestige that George brought her to Harlem.

In Harlem, Constancia had found her paradise. The oil-wells of Oklahoma were the open-sesame for which the portals of that extensive domain which goes by the name of Harlem society had swung wide to her. Wherever she went she conquered, and her weapons were various and well selected. Her interest in social activities won over the doctors' and lawyers' wives with whom, as Dr. Brandon's wife, she must naturally spend a part of her time; her democratic treatment of actors, writers, and singers made them her devoted slaves, while the very first week she was in New York her astounding vivacity and bewildering language completely floored Mrs. Vanderbilt-Jones of Brooklyn, who sent her an invitation to the Cosmos ball, and who even consented in all her rippling glory of black silk spangled with jet to attend Constancia's first Sunday night at home. For six days Harlem buzzed with the astonishing sight of Mrs. Vanderbilt-Jones in an animated and gracious conversation with Lottie

Smith, singer of blues. Constancia had indeed been more than conquerer.

The Brandons purchased a fourteen-room house in what was called by less-moneyed, and perhaps slightly envious, Harlemites, Striver's Row. George, who, despite the unceasing emissions from the Oklahoma wells, came of industrious stock and willed to be a capable practicing physician, was relegated to the ground floor, while Constancia ruled supremely over the rest of the house.

She was endowed with taste of a diffusive sort, which communicated itself to the furnishings of her home as well as to her guests. What money could secure she bought, but indiscriminately. A survey of her home found ages and periods and fadistic moments juxtaposed in the most comradely and unhistoric manner, while the contributions of countries were wedded with the strictest disregard for geography.

Constancia never moved an eyelash to corral, but every author who came to her home either brought or sent an autographed copy of his books. Constancia dutifully and painstakingly read them all, after which she would give George an intricate *résumé* (which he promptly forgot) in order that, should he ever emerge into society, he might converse with intelligence, and while talking to

Bradley Norris not compliment him on the beauty of a poem which had been written by Lawrence Harper. No artist or singer was permitted to plead fatigue or temperament at Constancia's *soirées*. He might offend once, but Constancia would remark within ample hearing distance that temperament was the earmark of vulgarity and incapacity. If the erring virtuoso sinned a second time, she blue-penciled him, and remembered him with an elephant's relentlessness. For this reason her innumerable parties never lacked excitement and verve, and there was seldom a week in which the *New York Era* or the *Colonial News* did not carry a portrait of "Harlem's most charming hostess."

Lest it be thought that Constancia was built along strictly frivolous lines, let it be noted in all fairness and in her defense that she found time to belong to sixteen lodges which she never attended, but in which she was never unfinancial, and at whose yearly women's meetings she was always called upon to speak. She was a teacher in the Episcopalian Sunday school, because it convened in the morning and so left her free for her afternoon visits and her Sunday-evening at-homes. She was a member of the Board of the National Negro Uplift Society and a director of the Diminutive Harlem Theatre Group; and she yearly donated fifty dollars for the best poem "by any poet," (never would she consent to stipulate "by any colored poet," although a colored poet had always won the award) published during the year in the *Clarion*, the Negro monthly magazine. Added to this, she belonged to two bridge clubs, one sorority, a circulating library, and she gave one hour a week in demonstrating household duties at the Harlem Home for Fallen Girls.

The freemasonry existing between the races in New York neither pleased nor disturbed her. She was equally gracious to an eccentric dancer from the Lafayette Variety Theater and to a slumming matron from Park Avenue, out with fear and trembling to discover just how the other color lived. When at one of her parties it was suggested to her in fiery language by a spirited young Negro, who could neither forget nor forgive, that a celebrated white writer present was out to exploit and ridicule her, she had replied:

"Ridicule me? If he contrives to depict me as I am, he shall have achieved his first artistic creation. If he does less, he shall have ridiculed himself. And besides, don't be so damnably self-conscious or you will be miserable all your life. Now vouchsafe me your attendance and let me introduce you to the ogre who has come to devour us all."

She had then taken the protesting youngster by

the hand, piloted him through her groups of chattering guests, and brought him to a standstill before Walter Derwent.

"My dear Mr. Derwent, I want you to do me a kindness. Here is a young man who is laboring under the apprehension that your frequent visits to Harlem have an ulterior motive, that you look upon us as some strange concoction which you are out to analyse and betray. I wish you would either disabuse him of, or confirm him in, his fears."

And she had left them together, both equally frightened.

After leaving them, she had paused to shout into Mrs. Vanderbilt-Jones' deaf and sparkling ear:

"I have just coupled a diminutive god with a sprouting devil." She had passed on before Mrs. Vanderbilt-Jones could summon courage enough to demand an explanation of the riddle.

Mattie had been Constancia's maid for over six years, six days out of seven. Being maid meant making herself generally useful, and giving orders to Porter, *l'homme à tout faire*, who was disinclined to see work which was not pointed out to him. Mattie adored Constancia, although she disapproved of her parties and thought her guests exceedingly strange and curiously mannered. Constancia spoke of Mattie as the perfect maid, a

jewel of the first water. She had reached this con-
clusion when, coming home one afternoon, she
had interrupted Mattie in the midst of her dusting, to inform her:

"Mattie, I have just been psychoanalyzed."

Mattie had said nothing for a moment, but had
ceased dusting, and had then delved down into
her apron pocket, whence she extracted a small
pocket dictionary. After turning its pages and
scanning the word carefully, she had turned to the
fascinated Constancia and, without a ripple stir-
ring her smooth black face, had said:

"Yes ma'am. I hope you liked it."

Constancia had flown to her, had kissed her,
and called her a *rara avis*, which had disturbed
Mattie throughout the day because she could not
find that in her dictionary.

Chapter Seven

WHEN, the morning after her decision to marry Sam, Mattie, who had been hovering around Constancia as she presided over the percolator, suddenly blurted out, "I should like to get the day off, Mrs. Brandon, after I do the dishes, for something very important," Constancia, whose wide eyes could express the utmost astonishment, while in reality nothing ever astounded her, exclaimed, "Whatever for?"

"To get married, ma'am."

Porter, who had been piling wood in the open fireplace, but who had been listening at the same time, stopped with open mouth. Constancia was unpleasantly alarmed.

"Whomever to?" she cried, and then, without giving Mattie a chance to reply: "Not to Porter, I hope. Tell me, child, have I been unwittingly fostering a romance under my roof which is going to cost me two good servants? For I could never have you both here. The house would go to rack and ruin while you osculated and doved all day long. Why don't you answer me? *Is* it Porter?

Porter married would be a calamity; he is slow enough now."

She turned to George, who was evincing a mild interest in the proceedings.

"Do you hear, George? Mattie wants to marry Porter."

Mattie finally interrupted.

"No, ma'am, it isn't Porter. His name is Sam."

Constancia sank back relieved.

"You need not bring the smelling-salts, Mattie, so long as it isn't Porter. Sam, at least, is a respectable Ethiopian cognomen. But you must tell me about him. Where did you meet him?"

"At the revival."

"At the revival? *Was* there a revival? What a place to meet a husband! This is bizarre!"

George, who after many years of married life had not yet become accustomed to Constancia's freedom of speech and inquiry, motioned her to cease bantering Mattie.

"I will not desist, George." Constancia drew a chair up for Mattie. "Sit down, dear, and tell me everything. *Tout, tout, tout!* Why, George, suppose I had been introduced to you at a revival instead of at the Alpha Phi Alpha dance, do you think I would have married you? Not for all the petroleum in Oklahoma."

George, confused and hurt, arose and kissed Constancia, then lumbered out of the room.

She followed him lovingly with her eyes, and while he was still within hearing distance confessed to Mattie, "Child, I would have espoused him had I encountered him at the Kitchen Mechanics' ball. Now let's revert to Sam. What's he like?"

Mattie, dreamy with the memory of the previous evening, of Sam's heavy proposal hastened by her will to have him, feeling still the hard strength of his arm about her, tasting still the cruel sweetness of his kiss, told how she had met him, how his conversion had conquered her hardness and brought her from sin to grace.

Constancia listened with eyes that were wide with a specious incredulity.

"But one arm, Mattie," she argued. "However will you manage with a husband lacking an appendage?"

"That doesn't matter, ma'am. I love him all the more for it; it will make him lean on me all the harder. And besides, that one arm is as strong as two."

"What you say may be perfectly true," Constancia agreed. "And really," she added, reflectively, "his deficiency might have been even more calamitous."

Constancia toyed with her coffee-cup and mused. Mattie was such a good girl and had been such a jewel of a maid. She would like to do something for her. Here was an opportunity to help her in a munificent way.

"What plans have you made for the wedding?" she asked Mattie.

"Oh, we haven't made any plans. Sam is waiting for me at the house. I told him I'd be there as soon as I could get away from here, and then we'd go and get the license together, and come back uptown and have Reverend Drummond marry us."

"Mattie"—Constancia leaned across the table, her gray eyes kindled with largesse—"you must let me marry you from here. You must let me supervise your wedding."

Mattie demurred, "I don't know how Sam would like it."

"He is only incidental, my dear. This is your wedding. You must let me handle it for you."

As if it were settled, Constancia went on, carried away by the prospect, "Is there anybody you would like to come, any special body?"

"No one but Aunt Mandy."

"Well, I'll send George along with you in the car. He can take you down to get the license, and then bring you and Sam and your Aunt Mandy to the house. I'll arrange with Reverend Drummond and invite the guests, just a few friends of mine, to liven up the proceedings. Tell me, Mattie, how do you feel about miscegenation?"

Mattie, who had been taken unawares, without her dictionary, could only gasp in complete ignorance, "About what, ma'am?"

Constancia was so completely enamored of what the day promised, that she condescended to an explanation.

"I mean, my dear, do you mind if I invite some white people to witness the ceremony?"

"Oh, I don't think I'd like that. I don't care much for white people."

"Well, that's very wrong of you. I had no idea you were prejudiced. Nevertheless, it shall be as you like. You are missing a splendid material opportunity, for Walter Derwent has coined enough money on his articles about us to afford a handsome donation to the gift-table. Now I'll call George and you can go see about the license. We'll set the wedding for five o'clock. But you return as soon as you secure the license, for I want to dress you here. Bring Sam and your aunt along with you, so there will be no danger of his changing his mind. I'll have the minister here. . . . George!"

In answer to Constancia's shrill summons,

George lumbered upstairs. "Darling, you will have to divest yourself of that badge of servitude," she said, pointing to the white coat he wore in his office, "and people who can't do any better will just have to die. You are having a holiday today. I am going to give Mattie away; that is I am going to have her married from here. I want you to take her and her husband-to-be down to the license bureau, and then bring them back here. Now run along. No, no, no. (Her negatives were like a dove's cooing, and each one was followed by a peck on George's lips.) No protestations. Run along."

As Mattie and George were leaving, Constancia suddenly remembered something. She ran to the door and poked her head out into the cold January air. Her earrings swung gayly.

"Mattie," she cried, "have we any rice?"

Mattie turned in bewilderment.

"Any rice, child, rice? You can't get married without rice. Oh, it's your wedding. How stupid of me to expect you to know what is needed! George, bring back some rice, about two pounds, superior quality."

Inside again, and seated at her desk, with a small golden pen poised over a white tablet, the telephone at her elbow, Constancia was so filled with plans that even she was at a loss where to begin.

She thought it might be best to make certain that the minister was unengaged for the hour agreed upon. She dialed.

"Is this the Mount Hebron Methodist Episcopal Church? . . . Give me Reverend Drummond, please. . . . This *is* Reverend Drummond? How stupid of me! I should have recognized your voice. This is Mrs. Brandon—Mrs. George Brandon. I want to tell you how sorry I was to miss your exquisite revival. I hear it was disconcertingly successful and that sinners were taken in by the hundreds. . . . What? there were only thirty-odd? Well, even that is encouraging. Small commencements sometimes make frightfully large endings. Do let me know when you are having another revival. I have so many friends who might profit by attendance. Now to the point at issue. Can you perform a wedding at my home this afternoon at five? I know you will be interested to learn that the contending parties are two of your converts—my maid Mattie and the one-armed man who discarded his cards and his razor. . . . You will come? . . . How sweet of you. At five, then. Good-by."

She dialed again.

"Mrs. Vanderbilt-Jones? . . . Dear, this is Constancia. I want you to drop everything you are doing and be at my house at five o'clock. Mattie is being married. . . . Who is Mattie? Why, my maid, the one who makes those delicious anchovy sandwiches that you like so well. Yes, you recollect her now? Well, there won't be any anchovy sandwiches today because I can't make them and Mattie is being married. But you will come, won't you? And bring a present, my dear."

She leaned back almost exhausted, but her Spartan courage could not be vanquished. When she had completed her calls she had exacted promises of attendance, with presents, from Lottie Smith, the blues singer; from Lawrence Harper, the poet; from Stanley Bickford, the architect; and from several less-prominent but socially important personalities. For a moment she toyed with the phone as if undecided about something which she very much wanted to do. Finally she yielded to the impulse and dialed.

"Mr. Derwent please. . . . Oh, Walter, this is Constancia. Listen, dear. My maid Mattie is being married today from my house, and I am calling on my friends to donate something to the gift-table. . . . Yes, the lovely little dark thing who serves so nicely, and who slapped your friend's face last time you were here when he attempted to kiss her. Served him right, too. Well, Walter, I want you to send something, something lovely as you always do; you know your taste is so irre-

proachable. Unfortunately, the child is prejudiced. . . . Yes, that's it, she has race prejudice
and simply refuses to have a black-and-tan wedding. So I can't invite you. . . . No, you *couldn't*
pass for colored. Don't be pretentious; she has
seen you too often. But you will send a present,
won't you. . . . That's lovely. And, Walter, if you
think it will console you any, you can read all
about it in next week's *Tattler*."

When George and Mattie returned, about two
hours later, with Aunt Mandy and Sam, Constancia was knee-deep in roses and ferns; six
canaries in beribboned cages were doing their in-
finitesimal best to add to the general derangement,
while two extra women, hastily summoned, were
busy in the kitchen. Constancia paused long
enough to give Sam an appraising and apprecia-
tive glance.

"He *is* good-looking," she whispered to Mattie.
"Now all of you run up to the top of the house
and sleep, play cards, bathe, or do whatever you
like, while I finish these nuptial trimmings."

The bell rang. Although it was only one o'clock,
Lawrence Harper, who adored Constancia and
who had been greatly intrigued by the invitation,
had come to see what assistance he might offer.
In his hand he held a package tied with blue-and-
red ribbon.

"For the bride and groom," he explained, handing the package to Constancia. "May they read and adore them."

"What is it?" asked Constancia.

"My poems, of course! I got them at the author's reduction rate."

"The poet's mite. How sweet of you! Well, just sit down somewhere and write another poem."

A messenger came in holding gingerly a large box which, when Constancia took it, was much lighter than it looked. Inside were twelve fragile gold-rimmed champagne glasses and Walter Derwent's card, inscribed, "To Mattie with lilacs and geraniums." Constancia held the glasses up to the light, where they sparkled anticipatingly. "Walter must have thought *I* was being married," she commented. "Next time I see him I'll make him supply that for which these glasses were intended."

At three Mrs. Vanderbilt-Jones drove up in suburban dignity, and in a taxi. She had bought a new ear-trumpet which she was clutching violently in one hand while in another she held a fair-sized package.

"Constancia," she complained, "I wouldn't have come for anybody but you. You have no idea how expensive it is to take a taxi from Brooklyn to New York. It's sheer banditry on the part of these taximen. The Subway is cheaper, of course, but so tedious and smelly."

"Have you ever tried the Paris metro, second class?" Constancia inquired.

"I have never tried anything second class—that is, to my knowledge. Here take this present. I hope you like it."

Constancia undid the package and discovered a beautiful porcelain vase. It was so lovely with its blue water and willow trees that she half envied Mattie for it.

"Ravishing," she said. "Is it Sèvres?"

"Certainly not," protested Mrs. Vanderbilt-Jones, petulantly detaching her veil, "It is Ovington's latest.

"Constancia," the old lady continued, settling herself comfortably where she would be most in the way, "come here and sit beside me for a moment. There, that's a dear. I have something of social importance to tell you. I am moving to Harlem. Brooklyn bores me. There is so much life here, and such smart people, and you. I am moving into a very select apartment in that new district known as Sugar Hill. I can't say that I think the name is at all dignified, nothing like *Brooklyn*, you know. But the houses are so lovely. All the white people are moving out, bless them, and only the best colored people are moving in—doctors and lawyers and teachers."

Constancia groaned audibly.

"I have the loveliest apartment," the dowager went on; "seven rooms completely overlooking the city. What a view! And just think, dear, *two bathrooms!*"

Constancia slid to the floor, to busy herself anew twining roses and ferns. Mrs. Vanderbilt-Jones waggled a dropsical finger at Lawrence Harper, but the bard refused to budge. The old lady closed her eyes and fell asleep thinking what temperamental people poets were.

Lottie Smith and Stanley Bickford came together at four. Stanley, tall, indolent, and so Nordic that he spent the major part of his time patiently explaining that he could look as he did and according to American standards be colored at the same time, brought a small parcel which gurgled when Constancia shook it.

"This I shall confiscate, Stanley," she admonished him. "I want these people to enjoy their honeymoon."

Lottie, whose boast was that she could put all the other Smiths to shame with her moaning, was slight, brown, and indescribably chic. She drew fabulous sums and spent them all on clothes; she always looked as if she had come directly from the rue de la Paix. She had burdened herself with two packages; both were circular, but one, wrapped in plain brown paper, was about five times the thickness of the other, which was encased in silver tissue, bound with ribbons of many colors.

Lottie was the only one who made Constancia gasp and stutter. She was so unlike what she ought to be; more like a successful business man's or a doctor's wife in appearance than like a blues singer.

"How Louise Boulanger you look today, Lottie, and how prodigal you are, and how like you to bring two presents!" Constancia complimented her.

"Well," boomed Lottie in that deep contralto voice worshiped from coast to coast, "they are all records—records of the St. Louis blues. These five (pointing to the somber package) are by my rivals. And this (holding up the festively decked disc admiringly) is by me. I want your maid to try these others first, and then I want her to play mine, and see how lousy the others are in comparison."

At this juncture Mrs. Vanderbilt-Jones, having sufficiently refreshed herself, descended upon Lottie to enchant her with the tale of the two bathrooms.

Constancia twined the last rose among the ferns with which she had draped the stairway down which Mattie was to come. She cocked her ear for a moment to see if above the profundity of Lottie's voice pouring into Mrs. Vanderbilt-Jones' trumpet, and over the clatter of a cocktail-shaker which Stanley was manipulating with affectionate and consummate artistry, while Lawrence stood near by, reading "*à haute voix*," his latest poem, she might not discover some coördinated melody in the abandoned rapture of the canaries.

She beamed upon them all, and excused herself.

"Enjoy yourselves in your several ways. I am going up to dress the bride."

Upstairs, she found Sam stretched out stomach down upon a sofa. His face was buried in his arm, while low staccato noises emanating from his direction demonstrated that he was sleeping the sleep of the weary and perhaps of the frightened, if not of the just. Aunt Mandy, arrayed in blue silk, was perched doll-like in a rocker, her small hands spread out on the arms of the chair, her little bird eyes contentedly contemplating her jewelry. The gold hoops were back in her ears. Mattie had drawn a chair up to the sofa, where she sat demure and brooding, keeping happy and guardian watch over Sam.

"Let him sleep," whispered Constancia. "He'll

merely have to lave his face afterwards, but you must hurry and get accoutered. You and your aunt come into my room while I transform you into a bride."

"I had planned to be married just as I am, ma'am." Mattie regarded her soberly-cut blue dress as if she found in it all the sartorial excellence necessary.

Constancia merely took her by the arm and drew her along, motioning to Aunt Mandy to follow. "My dear," she said, "this is the one occasion on which you must look your supremest, no matter how dowdy you may become afterwards. One's marriage is not a quotidian affair. I want Sam to be overcome by your loveliness when he sees you, asphixiated, as it were. I want him to think you are a butterfly which has broken its chrysalis and flown straight to him. Men like finery and pretty things on a woman—our men, especially. There's nothing to retain them like a splash of color, or a gold tooth, or some beads around the neck. I have set my heart on having you wear these things. Look!"

She held up the dress; it was cherry-colored; to Mattie's touch it was softer than the stuff of a spider's web. On the floor were a pair of slippers, a darker crimson, with tiny black-velvet bows.

"They're lovely!" Mattie exclaimed. "But I

couldn't wear them; they wouldn't go with my color. It's much too red, and I'm too dark."

"Nonsense!" Constancia reassured her. "There's not a lovelier combination than black and red. Just try them on for me."

Mattie allowed herself to be persuaded, and when, after a bit of tucking and pinning to make the dress fit her, she stood before the mirror and looked at herself, and then gazed down to where her little feet peeped out as if half afraid to issue forth in their finery, she was incredulous of her loveliness. Aunt Mandy could only stand off, and then circle her, her hands clasped in admiration, her tongue clucking excitedly as if she were a bantam hen calling her brood.

"Now sit down and compose yourself," Constancia urged Mattie, "while I get dressed."

After Constancia had arrayed herself in a clinging gray dress relieved by a large green brooch, and had changed her swinging gold earrings for others which were longer and which sparkled with small green stones, she descended to see what other arrivals had come while she had been occupied with Mattie.

She found Reverend Drummond in animated conversation with Stanley. "But the church is necessary even to an architect," the minister was saying, while Stanley's childish blue eyes were staring with polite attention but with scant conviction.

Dr. and Mrs. Wilbur Roach had arrived; and Counselor and Mrs. Geoffrey O'Connell, while aloof and to themselves, as if hatching a plot, were the society editors of the *New York Era*, the *Colonial News*, and the *Tattler*. There were two new gifts on the table—a samovar from the Roaches and an envelope from the O'Connells, probably a check, for the slight, monocled lawyer was sure to donate something practical.

"I'm so glad to see you, Reverend." Constancia tendered the pastor a heavily-ringed hand. "We'll be ready in just a moment."

She looked across at Stanley and saw the pleading in his eyes; she had compassion for him. She remembered that he had wanted to be a concert artist before veering off to architecture, and that in his long drink-nervous fingers there still resided a magnetism that could draw harmony from a piano as the magnet draws the nail. "Stanley," she said, in her most improvising tone, "I wish you would play for us, Mendelssohn or Wagner, when Mattie starts down the stairway. You might go over to the piano now and limber your fingers up."

Darting her beams of affectionate gratitude, he scuttled to the piano, where his fingers arabesqued across the keys in the sheerest ecstasy of deliverance.

Reverend Drummond gazed fondly after him.

"A fine young man, a splendid architect, I've been told, a real credit to the race," he growled, "but terribly misguided. He has no religious affiliations. I should like to talk to him sometime and put him on the right track."

"I'll bring him to your next revival," promised Constancia. Then raising her voice and addressing them all, "I shall send the groom down now."

She floated upstairs. Sam had washed the sleep from his eyes, and was pacing the room nervously when she entered. George sat moodily in a corner, silently anathematizing Constancia and her mad whims, but letting his devotion for her show all too plainly in his eyes as she rustled into the room.

"It'll soon be over," she consoled Sam. "Take him downstairs, George. They are waiting."

"But where's Mattie?" Sam was not accustomed to pre-marital etiquette, and he had been apprehensive since he woke up to find Mattie gone.

"Oh, she's about," Constancia assured him; "she'll just be fashionably tardy."

As he encountered the unfamiliar faces in the drawing-room, Sam let all the boldness of his gaze go out and affront them. They were not of his world. They had what he hadn't and didn't want—

money and schooling; they were society. He eyed them insolently, not bending his head when they bowed to him, raging inwardly as he saw them gaze in astonishment at his lonely arm. What a fool he had been to let this girl drag him here into this marriage.

Lottie Smith, to whom social status was unimportant, in view of the number of Harlem ladies to whom she was *persona non grata*, save when on the stage or when they were seeking a benefit performance for some one of their numerous charity enterprises, went over to Sam. "Let me congratulate you," she said. "Mattie is such a pretty girl."

Mrs. Vanderbilt-Jones, who often disconcerted people by hearing what she was supposed to miss, jerked the blues-singer by the sleeve. "I think you are a bit premature, Lottie," she warned. "Congratulations are due after the ceremony."

Just then Constancia's ivory face appeared at the head of the stairs, thus terminating what might have been a warm argument endangering the friendship of the dowager and the cantatrice. A gem-studded finger was crooked into a signal for Stanley who launched forth into the "Lohengrin Wedding March," while Sam looked up to behold a rapturous vision.

His heart spurted like a fountain within him, sending strong currents beating for release in the palm of his hand, in his ears, and in the somber veins of his temples. Here was the vision which he had seen at the Communion table, but a reality far more ravishing than the dream. Mattie in a bright-red dress, her small dark feet encased in crimson slippers with black-satin bows! Her hair was curled and glossy. A sheaf of roses was in one arm. Her arms made music as she descended the stairs, for as she walked, the thin silver bracelets which Constancia had loaned her jangled and exulted. Her face, enkindled with happiness, rose up above the bouquet like a larger flower for which these others were only a setting, like an animated black tulip, rich and smooth and velvety.

Oh, I will love her and be kind to her and never leave her, Sam promised himself as he thought of his vision and of the black young fellow whose one arm boasted the strength of two. Behind her came Aunt Mandy and Constancia.

Reverend Drummond stood before them with open ritual. George stood at Sam's side, Aunt Mandy at Mattie's, and just in back, jubilant and serene, was Constancia.

"Have you a ring?" the minister asked Sam.

"No." Sam's great shame was in his voice.

"I have a ring," said Mattie. She turned to Sam and gave him her flowers to hold. "It was my mother's." She untied her handkerchief and extracted a plain gold band.

"With this ring I thee wed, and with my worldly goods I thee endow." Sam repeated the words after the minister, feeling small and cheap within himself as he realized their hollow unimportance. He was bringing her nothing but himself, a liar, cheater, professional religionist. But he would make amends. He would be good to her. He would find work and slave, and save, and keep her as the minister had said, "for better, for worse; for richer, for poorer; in sickness and in health," till death should part them.

"I now pronounce you husband and wife. Those whom our God has joined together let no man put asunder."

Forgetful and scornful of his surroundings, Sam encircled Mattie with his arm. Kissing her, he murmured, "Baby, baby!" while she leaned against him with closed eyes, time and space, guests and surroundings, outdistanced by her happiness.

"Let me congratulate you, Mrs. Lucas." The minister was holding out his hand, stiffly and with ceremony. But Constancia would not have it so. She was gay and happy; the wedding had been a ripping success; she could see the long columns in the *New York Era* and the *Colonial News*; she already saw by faith her picture in the next issue of the *Tattler*, and the caption: "Harlem's most charming and original hostess has magnificent" (the word would certainly be *magnificent*) "wedding for her maid." She was supremely blissful.

"Everybody osculate!" she cried, clapping her hands.

And lest she might not be understood, she leaned over and kissed Sam full on the lips. He stood stiff with rage and resentment, which was not lessened when the minister, after much cajoling by Constancia, pecked Mattie lightly. The women all kissed Sam, with much laughter and coyness, to his infinite disgust and helplessness. Mattie graciously entered into the sport, although it was of no import to her that she was being kissed by one of the famous poets of her race. What mattered was that she would be kissed by Sam over and over again. When Stanley Bickford approached with his blond hair rising in military precision, his fair face flushed, and his blue eyes anticipating the reward of his playing, Mattie drew back from him and looked appealingly at Constancia.

"My dear," said Constancia, with a trace of hurt in her voice, "do you think I would betray you? He's *colored*."

Mattie suffered herself to be kissed.

Reverend Drummond could not be persuaded to remain for the supper. He was wary of these people. He was sure there would be dancing and he felt there were liquors on the table. He had seen Stanley cache the cocktail-shaker as he entered, although it had been too late to conceal the glasses. He drew up the marriage certificate for Mattie. It was a large shiny paper somewhat resembling a diploma, but less severe. On it were roses, and a huge silver bell to ring in all the joys of their matrimonial life. At the bottom there was the picture of a book, open and lined; this was for the signatures of the witnesses. Everybody wanted to sign, and as there weren't lines enough, the names were allowed to spread riotously outside the book.

"It reads like the Social Register of Harlem," commented Constancia as she signed with a flourish.

After he had given Mattie her certificate and had pocketed his fee, the minister left, firmly refusing Constancia's entreaties to "stay for a bit of collation." As the door closed behind him, Stanley rushed to the piano, where he began to play the slow, sorrowful, almost religious strains of a blues. The music invaded Sam until he forgot his alien dislike for these people. He seized Mattie and swung her off into a dance. For a moment it was so blissful to feel his arm about her, and to sense his hot and desirous breath upon her cheeks, while his fine dark eyes unleashed their full power on her, that she allowed herself to float away in his arm. But suddenly she remembered certain mystic symbols tied up in a white handkerchief and hid away; her mind slid back to the white altar with the bowed repentant heads circling it; she thought of the dark, sinful hands faltering out for bread and wine. She stiffened in his arm.

"Sam, Sam," she whispered, "we're church members now. This isn't right. These things don't belong to us any more."

Her protest filled him with doubts and suspicions; small currents of remorse, ever widening and gathering strength, ran through him and shocked him. Had he, after all, chosen the better part? Was his own trickery to come back upon him like a boomerang, separating him from that felicity toward which he had dreamed in taking this woman? Was her religion, rooted and grounded in him, to be a barrier between them?

"Let's don't think of that now," he entreated. "Let's only think of bein' glad and happy; let's only think of lovin' each other." He held her more tightly, laughing at her half-hearted struggles, melting his will and his love into her, striving against the Holy Ghost, and conquering. Her taut body relaxed; she flung her head back until he had to brace his arm to hold her.

"All right," she assented, "let's only think of love tonight and of being happy. Play something fast," she cried to Stanley.

As the music quickened its pace the crimson slippers flashed in and out joyfully, the web-soft, cherry-colored dress whirled and flashed, its folds flaring out like the dress of a ballet-dancer. God! but she was a dancer, Sam thought. Elation filled his breast, and his mind romped ahead to other dances to come. Aunt Mandy, who could find good in cards and fortune-telling, hated dancing and drinking. She sat back in a chair and shut her eyes to blot out the abomination. The other guests formed a cordon around them, urging them on, with clapping hands, time-tapping feet, and those short, spontaneous cries which are the Negro's especially copyrighted expressions of delight. Sam and Mattie broke away from one another; they improvised; they strutted and glided, approached one another and backed away, did as much of the cake-walk as they could remember, and cast in for good measure all the dead-gone and buried steps of Negro dancing which came to mind: they shuffled, balled the jack, eagle-rocked, walked the dog, shimmied and charlestoned, till, breathless and riotously happy, they could only lean panting against each other, in blissful exhaustion.

"Bravissimo!" approved Constancia. "Now on to the viands." She threw out her hands and herded them into the dining-room as if she had been a farmer shooing chickens. Constancia was known as a bountiful hostess; the table, loaded with chicken salad, cold ham and tongue, olives, celery, pickles, and hot, buttered rolls, evidenced her decision not to imperil her reputation. Eggnog frothed in a bowl in the center of the table. Mattie caught Aunt Mandy's scandalized eye, and refused to drink, despite Sam's tender entreaties. But when Porter ambled in with iced bottles at the sight of which Mrs. Vanderbilt-Jones forgot her dignity to the extent of exclaiming, incredulously, "Champagne!" Mattie refused to look at her aunt. The pop of the bottles fascinated her, and the sparkling liquid became one final irresistible sin which she would commit on this night of love. She lifted her glass with the rest.

"Skoal!" cried Constancia.

"Buvons!" exhorted Stanley.

"To Mattie and Sam!" said Lawrence. The liquor had made him prosaic; he had wanted to say something in rhyme, but it wouldn't come.

Mattie tasted her drink and made a wry face; she didn't like it. She set the glass down, but Sam picked it up, kissed the rim where her mouth had been, and drained it.

"How romantic! How perfectly like a lover!" Mrs. Vanderbilt-Jones said, with glistening eyes. "It all takes me back to my marriage with Mr. Vanderbilt-Jones. If he were only living to be here with me now! My dear," she said, turning to Mattie, "you will remember this day when you are like me." Her voice trailed off in revery, her thought sank back into her slightly reeling brain.

But Stanley finished it for her, *sotto voce,* to Lottie, "Yes," he mocked, "with an ear trumpet, and two bathrooms on Sugar Hill. May Heaven forbid!"

Suddenly Constancia remembered something. She rushed up to Mattie in agitated inquiry. "Where are you honeymooning?"

Mattie laughed. "I hadn't thought of that."

Sam fidgeted uneasily, and cursed Constancia for a meddling fool.

"We're not going away," explained Mattie. "I've got to keep my work, and Sam has to find a job."

"But there must be a honeymoon," insisted Constancia, "of some sort. No wedding is complete without one. Why not go to a theater?"

Sam liked the idea; shows always pleased him.

"Where?" he asked.

"Some place downtown," said Constancia, "to one of the smart revues." She flicked back her sleeve and looked at her watch. "No, time has overruled that suggestion. It's already eight-thirty."

"Well, we could go to a colored show," said Sam. "I'd like it much better, anyhow." He hated to relinquish the idea, and he was anxious to get Mattie away to himself. "The Sable Steppers are at the Lafayette."

"Just the thing, the physician's very prescription," agreed Constancia. "I'll phone for a box for you; you just have time to make the nine-o'clock show. Porter can drive you over and then I'll see that your aunt gets home safely."

As Sam and Mattie were leaving, George came in with a huge pan of rice into which the guests delved; they threw the rice after the departing pair with spirited but inaccurate aim, and with small concern for the cracks and crevices in Constancia's house.

From her doorway Harlem's most ingenious hostess watched her car round the corner. The wedding had been most successful. She stooped and gathered up a few grains of the rice which lay on her brownstone steps like hard snow.

"Hail to Hymen!" she sighed as she sallied back to her guests.

ONE WAY TO HEAVEN

PART TWO

Chapter Eight

LIFE for the moment seemed more fine-favored and worth living to Sam than ever before. He took his awakening the next morning as a prelude to what the whole of his days to come would be. He had not felt Mattie shift her head from the crook of his arm, and it was with a somnolent surprise that, answering a tug at his sleeve, he looked up with puckered brow to find her bending over him. The ripples in his forehead receded into the smoothness of understanding as remembrance of last night began slowly to flood his brain. Although he closed his eyes sharply to give the dream, if it were a dream, time to abandon him, when he opened them again Mattie was still there. He turned and sat up, taking in anew the four close walls, the bedroom so tiny that two abreast could scarcely pass between the bed and the wall. He leaned over and sent the window shade swirling up so that the faint apology for sunlight which trickled in from the airshaft might bathe the room in its grayness, more like the light of early evening than of broad day. He wondered what time it was, and whatever time it might be, he hoped Mattie wouldn't want him to get up so early; he hated early rising. He yawned and stretched his hand up, vigorously shaking the sleep out of it.

Mattie sat down on the side of the bed and leaned over against him.

"Lazy?" she accused him.

"No, tired."

"Tired?" Mattie shunted back with lifted eyebrows and arms akimbo in an attitude of mock incredulity. "Tired of what?"

He eased down into the sheets again, from where he looked up at her with squint-eyed playfulness. "You ought to know, Mrs. Lucas," he said. "You know," he went on, avoiding the light tap she aimed at him, "I was 'fraid to open my eyes at first; thought last night and the days before might 'a' been nothin' but a dream. But here's you and here's me." He sat up again and surveyed his kingdom, "And here's home."

He noticed for the first time that she was fully clothed, dressed in a tailored suit the somber cut and dark hue of which contrasted sharply with the cherry-colored dress in which he had last seen her.

"Why'd you get up so early and dress?" he protested.

"It isn't early. It's eight o'clock. Time working-people were up and about. You know, Sam, there's no rest for the weary. I've got to get Mrs. Brandon's breakfast this morning same as every other one."

"But the honeymoon ain't over yet, honey. We ain't used up even a quarter of it." He pulled her down to him and kissed her. "A quarter did I say?" He smacked his lips. "We ain't even started to nibble on that moon."

Mattie ran her fingers through his hair; it wasn't easy going, for the pomade with which he had plastered it for his wedding, until it glistened like black satin, had dried, and the hard knotty curls had reverted to type until they were now a mass of little tight balls, like a patch of dwarfed and withered black grapes.

"No," Mattie mused. "You're right, honey boy, we haven't even started to nibble. We haven't even bit down hard into it; we've only drawn our tongues across it, scraped it with our teeth and tasted the sugar to make sure it was there. And now that we know it's there, if we just nibble a bit day by day, we'll have that honeymoon for mighty nigh forever. Ain't that better than just swallowing the whole cake today and snuffing ashes tomorrow? At any rate, thinking about it that way makes it easier for me to leave you and go off to work."

She stood up, smoothing her dress, as she continued, "But I thought you ought to have your breakfast before I go, and I've got it all fixed."

He made to get up, but she pushed him back gently. "No, this morning you're going to eat in style, served in bed with brown-skin service, or near-brown, anyway. I made up my mind long ago that I'd bring my husband his first breakfast to bed, that is, unless I happened to marry a man with money. Then, of course, we'd both have breakfast in bed."

"Well," Sam laughed, "that's one fine dream all shot to pieces."

She brought him water in a basin and washed his face in spite of his protestations; and then on a tray orange-juice, coffee, scrambled eggs, bacon, and toast. "I'm giving you just what Dr. and Mrs. Brandon will have this morning," she told him, pridefully, "unless it's a bit of brandy which they take in their coffee sometimes. And of course"— she waved her hands airily in summary dismissal of the thought—"you wouldn't want that, anyhow."

"No, I wouldn't want that, anyhow," Sam echoed, so slowly that she laughed in spite of her disapproval that he should really have wanted brandy.

She sat and watched him eat, saying that she

would snatch a bite for herself at Mrs. Brandon's. He took it as his due that she should so serve him, the circumstances being what they were. He told himself that after she had gone, and after he had caught up a bit on his sleep, he would get up and go out and try to find a job. He was genuinely excited at the prospect of a steady job, something to which he had not allied himself for many years.

After Mattie had gone, he lay gazing up at the ceiling and smiling, thinking how strange and fine it would be for him to be coming home on Saturday nights with money in his pockets and a little present for Mattie. Not that he would bring her his envelope unopened; he wasn't that kind of a man. A man should always be the boss in his home, he felt, and should open and pull the purse strings as he willed. The man ought to be head of the house. Well, he *would* be as soon as he had a job.

He turned over on his side and drew the covers more closely about him. Blazes! but it was cold; too cold to think about getting up for a while. Maybe Aunt Mandy would have a good hot fire burning when he did get up. He hoped she would. If there was one thing which he hated worse than getting up early, it was getting up in a cold room.

When he awoke again it was well after noon and the January sun had waxed so strong that a sliver of cold sunlight had come down the shaft and now adorned his bed with a spot of imitation warmth. He could hear a rustling and to-do in the kitchen. The power of strong black coffee invaded his nostrils, seeped down into his abdominal regions, and made him aware of a new hunger. Must be Aunt Mandy getting lunch, he told himself; well, it couldn't be ready any too soon for him.

Aunt Mandy was frying chops when he came into the kitchen. Fork poised lightly in hand, she welcomed him with an enthusiastic grin. She was a bit put out that she had been asleep when Mattie left and so hadn't been able to banter her; but she thought to take it out on Sam. She curtsied to him in mock reverence, and set her small, black, tantalizing eyes full on him.

"Good mornin', son. Sleep well?" The intonation of her query gave every indication that a negative response was expected.

But Sam was feeling shy and reserved. "Like a top," he said.

The little old lady was highly amused. She shook the long glistening fork, with which she had been probing the chops, at him, and wagged her head. "You tellin' me that and expectin' me to believe it? Lord! boy, see any green in my eyes? Think you can buy me for a fool?" She pulled the skin down from her eye and rolled her eyeball back until only the clear white shone out at him.

"Like a top, indeed!" she snorted, and Sam burst out laughing in spite of his embarrassment.

"Ben's been gone a long time," she said, looking past the chops and past Sam and past time into the past. "But I still know there's nothin' like bein' married and lovin' one another." She brushed the moisture away from her eyes and attacked the chops with renewed vigor, "Now ain't I becoming the sentimental old fool, with Ben dead and gone all these years and me gettin' moony about him now!"

"You was plumb sweet on him, wasn't you, a'nty?" Sam was leaning indolently against the kitchen door like some sleek two-legged animal. His gaze took in the kitchen and Aunt Mandy; if he turned his head he could see from where he stood the snug living-room, and leading from it the pitifully small hall, their foyer. It all seemed very natural to him, as if he had been holding on to some slender string all his days, winding it carefully around his hand, holding his breath lest it might break and the severed skein be swept away in the wind. Life was a silken thread which he had succeeded in holding on to until it had brought him here. Now he could throw it away; let the wind take it; let it go. His traveling days were done.

"I was gone on him for twenty years." He had

forgotten Aunt Mandy for the moment, and her high-pitched voice brought him back with a jerk from his dreaming. "Son, you'll never know what real livin' is until you've lived out rain and shine, good times and bad, sickness that's just around the corner from dyin', and everything that makes up life with one person, like I did with Ben for twenty years. Even now I can't think of him without this crazy feelin' here; and when I go to meetin' and they start talkin' about heaven, sometimes I don't know which one I want to see first when I get over there, Jesus or Ben."

"He must 'a' been awful good to you a'nty."

"Well, he was just a man, son, no better than most of you. Any woman what gets one of you ought to know before she takes you that mostly she's takin' a bundle of trouble—sweet, sweet trouble." Her eyes frolicked at the memory of the pain and worry Ben had caused her, and her flat withered bosom heaved a sigh of regret that it was not all to be borne again.

"You know, a'nty"—they were seated at the table, where Sam was enjoying his lunch as much as if breakfast had never been—"I feel about Mattie the way you did about Ben, only more. I'm so sweet on her that all the fine times I had before I met her, all the times that seemed so swell then, don't seem like nothin' now. I feel like I know what the preachers means when they says you must be born agin. You watch and see how little trouble I'm goin' to give her. I'm goin' to be so good to her she's goin' to have to beg me to stop."

"You is, son?" She was all unconcealed merriment and disbelief. "I hopes so. But that's honeymoon talk you doin' now. I hope to God it don't run out. My Mattie's the stickin' kind, and whenever she goes into anything she goes in for keeps."

She leaned over to pour him another cup of coffee; her wee inquisitive face peered up almost beneath his nose as she asked him, so abruptly that he drew back in dismay, "When you thinkin' about findin' a job?"

The question was distasteful to him at the moment. He was feeling so prime and well-nourished, slightly sleepy again. He thought a nap now might do him good. But, no, he had to go to work; he wasn't a rounder any more. He was a married man. His wife was pretty. How pretty he knew, as he remembered how people had looked at her at the theater the night before. As they had taken their seats, one coffee-colored rowdy, overcome by the cherry dress and Mattie's piquant black face, had exclaimed, "Must be recess up in heaven; they's let an angel out." And Sam had not been offended, but had grown cocky like a rooster, proud of the envious eyes upon him.

After the theater he had had to beg long and ardently before Mattie would consent to go to the Savoy for a little dancing. She had said it wasn't right for church members; but he had argued that church members weren't held accountable for a little sinning on their wedding night. Finally she had gone with him, and how she had danced! How washed out and faded the yellow and light-brown hostesses had appeared in comparison with her. He had seen more than one man, taking his ten-cent dance with one of these girls, pause and lose his step looking at Mattie. And what a tremendous joy it had been for them to scorn a taxi and to walk home after the dance, his arm supporting her, infused with the strength of two arms now by the full tide of possession. Yes, he must find something to do.

"I'm aimin' on goin' out huntin' for somethin' this afternoon, a'nty. What you think a man like me can find to do? What kind of a job you think they got for one-armed people?"

"What sort of a job did you have last?"

"The last steady job I had was helpin' paw on the farm."

"Well, they ain't no farms up here." He could sense her disapproval of his period of idleness. "We got to think of somethin' else. You couldn't be no policeman. It would be nice if you could be a policeman."

"We better rule that out, a'nty; that's the one thing I couldn't be."

"And you couldn't be a fireman, could you?"

"No, a'nty, I ain't never heard of no one-armed fireman; they ain't that hard up. We better think about somethin' simpler than that."

"You know I'm sorry about that, Sam"—she was very wistful and regretful. "I'd like so much for you to get a job where you had to wear a uniform. I think you'd look grand, you're so nice and tall."

"How about an elevator job in one of these dicty apartment-houses? I might get somethin' like that. That would mean a uniform all right. I'll go out in a little while and see what I can find."

But when he crossed over to the window and looked out through the frosty pane, the sight of the few people outside scurrying past with their coats tightly drawn about them and their coat collars turned up transmitted to him a feeling of how cold it must be out there, and reassured him how good it was to be inside where there was a fire. He shook his head, and went and sat down before the stove, where his full stomach and the heat sent him off into a quick doze. When he awoke, blinking his eyes against the light which the early darkness had caused Aunt Mandy to switch on, he could see heavy flakes of snow hurtling past on the outside. He couldn't find a job in weather like this. He could smell the supper simmering in the kitchen. At the table, with her back toward him, Aunt Mandy was busy telling her cards. He got up and went over to her.

"What they sayin' today, a'nty?"

"They ain't sayin' much today. Can't seem to make any sense out of them; they get like that some time, get just honery and cussèd, like people."

"See any job in them for me?" He wanted her to know that he really meant to work and that a job lay very heavily on his mind.

"I wasn't tryin' to find that out." There was a faintly disapproving note in her tone. "But I guess there's a job for any man what gets up and looks for one."

"Don't worry, a'nty," he placated her, patting her on the back. "I'll find something to do. It just takes time."

He leaned over and took up the cards which she relinquished. "Do you know any games to play with these? Somethin' you and me could play to make the time go quicker? I wish to God Mattie was here."

She was mollified now, but reluctant. "I ain't accustomed to playin' card games, but I did used to play casino with Ben sometimes. You know that one?"

"Yes, I know that one, but it ain't very excitin'. Can you play coon can?"

"What on earth is that?"

"It's a game where you make 'leven cards out of ten."

"Now, son, you know they ain't no truth in that. How you goin' to make 'leven cards out of ten?"

"Well," he laughed at her, drawing his chair up more closely, "that's the secret. Some coons can and some can't. Here's one what can."

"Can what, boy?" She was immensely flattered that he was willing to take up his time with her, and she had already forgiven him for not having gone in search of work. She was even ready now to say a good word for him should Mattie censure him.

"Play coon can," he answered, and they both fell to laughing with that heartiness with which Negroes laugh at anything which they feel worth being merry over.

She was an apt pupil, and before the afternoon was ended he had let her win several games so as to keep her feeling kindly toward him. He even succeeded in teaching her to play black-jack, although he experienced a bit of a problem here, for she found it difficult to count and seemed bent on forgetting that face cards valued ten. He persuaded her into adding to the excitement of the game by dividing a box of matches between them; they used these for chips, and when the game was ended, after two hours of playing, he had let her win every match. His difficulty in holding his cards, because of his one arm, amused and charmed her. She laughed that he should place his cards on a chair drawn up beside him, and pushed under the table out of her sight, leaning down to fish one out whenever it became his turn to play. She was delighted with him. And he felt warm toward her and knew that he would always have an ally in her.

When they had finished playing, he set the table for her. It was awkward for him, but he felt that in doing it he was diminishing any criticism which might be directed to him on the score of idleness. Then he sat down before the fire again and thought of Mattie. She would soon be in. She generally came in about six, Aunt Mandy told him.

How he hated this weather. He surely would be glad when it began to get warm and a man could go out and enjoy himself instead of moping around the house. If it hadn't been for the snow, he might have had a job by now, for it had been his absolute intention to look for a job after his nap this afternoon. He hoped Mattie would understand. Tomorrow the snow would be over, no doubt, and he could go out and look for something. He dozed off again.

Chapter Nine

It is very strange that in the home of an American Negress (if I used this designation in the presence of any of my colored friends any place except in Constancia Brandon's drawing-room, I should be drawn and quartered immediately, although I cannot see why) I should find the one bit of atmosphere which reminds me of England. Her *salon* is every bit like a patch of Hyde Park dug up and transplanted to America; it is the one place in which the vaunted Yankee freedom of speech and thought are really given full leeway. Here one says what he thinks, and whether it be boresome, brilliant, or brutal, his right to say it is seldom challenged.

WHETHER this extract from a letter written by Donald Hewitt to his mother was fully comprehensible or merely scandalous to that Victorian lady is beyond the point. What is true is that what this tall, finger-snapping, yodeling Englishman avowed in writing, all Harlem that mattered, and much of colored Baltimore, Washington, and Philadelphia, admitted tacitly. Constancia's monthly *soirées*, held the first and third Mondays in each month (June, July, and August excluded), were as analogous to a gala grand-opera performance as the Lord's prayer done on the head of a pin is similar to the same petition prepared for the naked and unembellished eye— that is, her *soirées* were far more interesting than the opera galas.

The joy and verve of these gatherings were cloaked under the uninviting and prosaic auspices of the Booklovers' Society, but it was known at large, and admitted by more than half the group itself, that they never read books, although now and then they might, under pressure, purchase the latest opus of some Negro novelist or poet. This was especially true in the case of the Negro members (the group was uncompromisingly interracial), who discovered, much to their chagrin, that the white members of the society were inclined to take Negro literature far more seriously than they. A case in point was Samuel Weinstein, the Columbia University student who was assembling a thesis on Negro writers; he not only bought and read books by Negroes, but had the embarrassing habit of remembering plots, authors' names, and isolated lines of poetry. He was a thorn in the flesh of most of the darker members of the society, for whom the chief *raison d'être* of Constancia's *soirées* was the impromptu program, the buffet collation, and the inevitable dancing which brought the evening to a close.

To give the devil his due, the Booklovers' Society at its inception had not belied its name. It had really been organized in the interest of books by and about Negroes, and in the fatuous conviction that the members of the society would live up to the obligations laid down for them in their constitution and by-laws, to wit: to buy and to read books by Negroes; to read (purchase optional) books about Negroes; *and to be a small but loyal body on which the Negro writer can depend for sympathy, understanding, and support.* Intelligent discussion of one book a month was inscribed as a basic tenet of the society.

When Constancia had first come to Harlem she had been aroused to the need of just such a society by repeated attendance at the monthly book discussion held at the local public library. She had found the meetings amiable, and a pure waste of time. There were seldom over twenty people present, and never more than five or six had read the book under discussion, although no one seemed to feel that the absence of even bowing acquaintance with the work should render him ineligible to criticize it. Constancia had finally wearied of the oft-repeated excuse, generally the prelude to an unintelligent tirade against the book, of, "I haven't read the book yet, but in view of what I have heard, I do feel that it should never have been published."

"What these people need," she thought, "is a real locale, a stimulus of lights and warmth; a cocktail before and after; and, when all the broadsides have been fired and friendships blasted, a bit of collation to lay the troubled waters."

Therefore quietly—though some in later embittered moments said slyly—so as to avoid the rabble, she made overtures to several of the more animate frequenters of the library symposium, with whom as a nucleus she formed her own Booklovers' Society. From the first the venture, small and select, was highly successful. The points of view represented were diverse and fractious. Miss Sarah Desverney, one of the local librarians, had risen to heretical heights and had forsaken the monastic coldness of the library meetings to warm her toes at Constancia's fire and the cockles of her throat with Constancia's wine; but she eschewed the heart of the fire. For her no Negro had written anything of import since Dunbar and Chestnutt.

Bradley Norris, to whom everything not strictly New Negro was anathema, was the bane and bait of poor Miss Desverney, to whom he took an unholy delight in reciting bits of *vers libre* and unconventional quatrains in which the Negro was depicted as being drunk with jazz and void of pudency. The antics of these two were a constant delight to the conniving Constancia.

Then there was Samuel Weinstein, bushy-haired and be-spectacled, serious in his native way, sincerely attracted to his Negro friends, yet never able to understand their lack of serious design. Because he could not reconcile a deficit of intent with Jewish consanguinity he had finally abandoned as untenable a long-cherished hope that the Negroes might be the strayed descendants of the lost tribe of Israel. As he never allowed his sincerity to be sullied with sentimentality, his caustic comments on Negro life, authors, and books were generally received in deferential and silent awareness of their truth, by all except Mrs. Harold De Peyster Johnson.

Mrs. Johnson was a teacher in the New York public-school system, and *ipso facto* a person of more than ordinary importance in Harlem Society. Her race consciousness dated back some seven or eight years. She had, as it were, midwifed at the New Negro's birth, and had groaned in spirit with the travail and suffering of Ethiopia in delivering herself of this black *enfant terrible*, born capped and gowned, singing "The Negro National Anthem" and clutching in one hand a pen, in the other a paint-brush. In the eyes of Mrs. De Peyster Johnson this youngster could do no wrong, nor had his ancestors ever been guilty of a moral lapse, or of an intellectual *faux pas*. Of misalliance, yes. This she sadly acknowledged as row after row of multi-colored faces, ranging from blackest jet to palest blond, and all representative of the young Hercules at whose shrine she worshiped, met her own dark countenance each morning. It was Mrs. De Peyster Johnson's boast that she was probably the one American Negro who could trace her ancestry back through an unbroken and unsullied line of Negroes straight to the first slaves landed in America.

"I find more to be proud of in that," she said, "than if they had come over on the *Mayflower;* for I don't believe the *Mayflower* had princes on it, while my ancestors were the blue-bloods of Africa. I am really one of the F. F. V.'s."

Mrs. De Peyster Johnson was certain that the Black Prince had been a Negro.

She carried in a worn and outmoded pocketbook, for the conversion of any disbeliever, a long strip of parchment on which her genealogy was traced in veracious black and white. Although she had not bothered to trace it farther than the Jamestown slaves, she was confident that if she cared to go to the trouble and expense, she could claim direct descent from the Queen of Sheba.

From among her suitors she had deliberately

rejected Thomas Asquith, who was sandy-haired, anemic, and scholarly, and toward whom she yearned in spite of herself; and had, with a true martyr's resignation and hope in the ultimate re- ward, married De Peyster Johnson, soot-colored, amiable, and totally lacking in interest and sym- pathy for the New Negro.

"There is something basically wrong and fore- boding," she thought, "in a Negro who is light- complexioned, sandy-haired, and named Thomas Asquith. It is evident at once that some one's brush-heap has been invaded. There might even be reason for questioning the racial purity of one named De Peyster Johnson; but one look at De Peyster is enough to convince any skeptic that his name is merely a matter of circumstance, instead of evidence of a skeleton on the family tree."

Fifteen years of slowly diminishing hopefulness with De Peyster had finally convinced Mrs. John- son that unbroken lines sometimes ended abruptly. In spite of prayers, candles to the Virgin and sundry saints; in spite of a visit to Rome, where she had kissed the toe of St. Peter's statue; in spite even of a bit of red flannel snipped from De Peyster's undershirt, dipped in asafetida and worn with cumulative courage around her neck, there was no junior De Peyster. Often at evening, sitting with stacks of papers before her, inspired essays sweated from forty-five youthful New Negroes, she would look up from her toil to cast a withering and malevolent gaze on De Peyster, who, with mouth open and fast-shut eyes, offered her his evening serenade from the parlor sofa. Her eyes would mist for a moment as her thoughts reverted to Thomas Asquith, by this time probably the sire of divers little sandy-haired New Negroes. She sometimes felt as if she could bear no more; but she always ended by putting the fox back into her bosom; she would cross the room, slap De Peyster's mouth shut, and return to her papers. The blue pencil would descend in tender correction upon some gross orthographical error, while the pale face and sandy hair of Thomas Asquith faded into limbo.

Mrs. De Peyster Johnson had emerged victorious from numerous clashes with her immediate superiors because of her set ideas as to just how and what the New Negro should be taught. Each morning she opened class with the singing of the Negro national anthem, while the afternoon dismissal was always preceded by a spiritual. Her young charges humored her and sang beautifully, but whispered among themselves that she was more unbalanced than inspired. She was once brought up on charges of evading the school curriculum, it being pointed out that while her pupils could recite like small bronze Ciceros, "I Too Sing America," and "Brother, What Will You Say?" they never had heard of "Old Ironsides," "The Blue and the Gray," or "The Wreck of the *Hesperus*." They could identify lines from Hughes, Dunbar, Cotter, and the multitudinous Johnsons, but were unaware of the contributions of Longfellow, Whittier, and Holmes to American literature. Their race-minded mentor finally bowed to the syllabus; but twice a week, with the aid of ice-cream and cake, and with the promise of Olympian leniency at the end of the semester, she cajoled her charges to her home, where she sang spirituals to them and taught them Negro literature. So strongly did she emphasize racial purity that the darker children were on the verge of becoming little prigs and openly snubbing their lighter-complexioned comrades.

With these, then, as the core,—Miss Desverney, Bradley Norris, Samuel Weinstein, Mrs. De Peyster Johnson, and a few kindred spirits, each acting as a foil or as a stick of dynamite to the other, as the case might be, the Booklovers had actually read and discussed books for at least six months. But the very ideals of bodily comfort on which Constancia had founded the organization effected its change from a small select society, with but a single aim, into a large polyglot group whose aims were legion. Gradually the little birds told, or the winds wafted rumors, of the cocktails with which the Booklovers' meetings were always opened, and of the irreproachable buffet suppers with which they ended. Close friends, pleading the privilege of their amity more than any literary proclivities, induced Constancia, whose warm heart could never resist an appeal that was insistent enough, to invite them "just this once." And like the worms in the ballad, they brought their friends, and their friends' friends, too, until Constancia was finally forced to make admittance to her *soirées* "by invitation only." By this time books had been relegated to that sphere in which most of the society thought they belonged—the lowest sphere of importance. Instead of literature, life written in major letters was dissected from all angles and with the utmost shamelessness. The cocktails were magical in loosening the most tightly nailed tongues, and Constancia's guests were soon discussing birth control, race suicide, the rise and fall of the French Cabinet, and whatever one word or another might lead to. Happy indeed was the foreign writer or the emancipated Southerner who came to Harlem looking for copy and who was fortunate enough to light on one of Constancia's evenings, and to be admitted. If he had his wits about him he could always leave with a story.

Sometimes, in their more sober moments, the protagonists in these chronicles deplored their wholesale distribution to the world, but more often they were proud to have figured in them.

Donald Hewitt's letter of praise to his mother had been occasioned by a happening which could of a truth have taken place in but one of two places—in Hyde Park or in Constancia's drawing-room. It was an unwritten rule of Constancia's that thoughts were sacred, though they might often be stupid, and that language, though it might not always be the king's, was the proper conveyance for thought. Therefore, in her drawing-room one might say, as he felt so disposed to say it, whatever he thought, and whoever was shocked or resentful immediately stamped himself as having wandered outside his intellectual milieu.

Donald was a young Englishman with charming manners, no prejudice, a great deal of money, and a misdirected desire to write. Since Donald was very anxious to do a book on America, and especially on Harlem, Walter Derwent, who piloted everybody who was not an out and out Negrophobe to Constancia's home, guided him to one of the meetings of the Booklovers.

"I am sure I shall love you people," Donald drawled, kissing his hostess' hand, and thereby causing her to doubt his nationality. "You have so much life and color about you, and you seem to enjoy yourselves so completely."

"Yes," assented Constancia, her ivory skin still tingling to the brush of Donald's lips. "*Carpe diem* is our motto."

"I am writing a book," Donald went on. "I have been writing one for years, but this one I shall surely finish. I am going to write about your people and dedicate it to you." (Had they been elsewhere in Harlem than in Constancia's home, Walter might have whispered to this novice in race relations that "your people" coming from white persons sets a Negro's teeth on edge. He was glad that at Constancia's race relations existed in theory only.)

"Walter chose a most opportune evening for your *début*," Constance informed Donald, with a smile. "You will probably learn a great deal about Negroes from one who has made a life study of them and who professes to know them better than they know themselves."

"Indeed!" the slightly nonplused son of Albion voiced his elation. "What did she mean?" he queried, as Constancia wandered off without having given any more detailed information, as was her dramatic custom.

"I don't know," said Walter, "but it will probably be a trump card when she plays it. Constancia rarely plays anything else."

But not even Walter Derwent, accustomed as he was to Constancia's boldness, had the remotest suspicion of the surprise which that eventful evening held in store. Indeed, the night at first gave every indication of petering out as nothing more than a social gathering at which a pleasant and boring time was enjoyed to the full. The attendance, to be sure, was record-breaking with people milling through the house in small gossipy groups as if they were on the scent of perfumed Easter eggs which had been carefully hidden away from them. Donald had drunk more than a score of cocktails which Mattie and Porter, both retained for these monthly gatherings, were dispensing with a prodigality shocking in a country addicted to prohibition. He was now a silent third in a conversation between Constancia and Miss McGoffin, an Irish-American missionary lady of abolitionist descent, whose aim it now was, since the American Negro had demonstrated the possibilities, to Christianize all Africa.

"Just see what Christianity has done for you people." Miss McGoffin let her eyes wander in approval over the appointments of Constancia's home. Her approbation suffered a slight curtailment as her gaze rested on the bare sepia-colored

back of Lottie Smith, whose robes were always cut
to show off to advantage what was to the unpreju-
diced eye a real adornment. "As I was saying"—
Miss McGoffin simply would not back water—"see
what Christianity has done for you people. I want
very much, when I return to Africa next month, to
take with me some message from their brethren on
this side of the water."

"You must give them our love," said Constancia.

"They will be so pleased," murmured Miss
McGoffin.

"And you must meet the duchess later on in the
evening, and Lady Hyacinth Brown," Constancia
added. "They will be sure to send even longer and
warmer messages."

"Duchess? Duchess?" Miss McGoffin was unde-
niably thrilled at the prospect.

"Yes," said Constancia, "the Duchess of Uganda,
née Mary Johnson. You'll love her "

"I'm sure I will," admitted Miss McGoffin.
"What people you do have, Mrs. Brandon! Tell
me now, coming back to my African charges—I
am trying to teach them spirituals. Of course they
have never had the proper incentive for them over
there, but you have no idea how they do rally to
the mood and tempo. Sometimes as I shut my eyes
over there in the African wilds and listen to them
sing your songs that I have taught them in my

poor way, I can fancy myself back in Georgia or Alabama or, or . . ."

"Or on Broadway?" suggested her hostess.

"Why, yes, to be sure," Miss McGoffin was more than agreeable. "What I want to know is, are you people writing any more spirituals? I should like so much to carry back a brand-new batch with me to show that civilization has not destroyed your creative instinct."

"Indeed!" said Constancia with apparent emotion on the subject. "Indeed we *are*; we almost had run out of them for a while, but plans are under way for a fresh supply at any moment."

"I am so glad," sighed the relieved Miss McGoffin. "I never tire of hearing them."

Just when Donald, damning first impressions, had sadly concluded that his hostess was as demented as her missionary guest, he was rewarded with what was without doubt a wink from Constancia's beautiful left eye. He sauntered off, eased of his fears, to join a rather largish group to which Bradley Norris was reading a poem. Miss McGoffin followed him and took a seat beside Stanley Bickford.

Bradley's poem was doomed, by the very nature of its perverseness, to be a failure. The poet felt like a renegade as he read it. Here was he, who had never stooped to rhyme before in all his youthful literary career, one both by sympathy and talent unmeet for the rigors of a sonnet, reading, with evident pride in his achievement, a sonnet, rhymed, metered, and allegorical. Let his comrades turn their heads in shame and cry, *"Et tu, Brute!"* They would learn in the fullness of time that he had merely done this to show the facility with which that sort of thing could be done, while a patternless poem made one sweat his very blood. It meant nothing to Bradley, and there was no one present sufficiently enlightened to tell him, that his rhymes were atrocious, that his meter limped, and that six of his lines were lacking in the proper number of feet which custom and decency have made indispensable to the sonnet. The message in itself was innocuous enough. Bradley had just discovered what every poet learns sooner or later, and the sooner the better, that the joys of the flesh are no less lovely than those of the spirit, and that the time allotted man for their enjoyment is infinitely more abridged. He looked like stout Cortes as he stood holding his bit of paper before him, declaiming in dulcet tones, if in poorer language, Herrick's advice to young men and maidens.

"Leave nothing for tomorrow; live today!" he fairly shouted the closing line in a frenzy of rapture and abandon.

"O tempora, O mores!" lamented the scandal-

ized Miss Desverney. "The poets of today are not those of yesterday. Dunbar would never have written anything as hedonistic and heathenish as that. You young poets are very glib in giving advice, but I wager you wouldn't want your sister to follow it."

"But I haven't got a sister," protested Bradley.

"That's just it," sniffed Miss Desverney, in triumphant rebuttal. "But if you had one . . ."

"I shouldn't bat an eyelash even if she married *white*," retorted Bradley.

Miss McGoffin touched Stanley Bickford on the arm. "That was a very lovely poem," she offered by way of commencing conversation, "but I didn't follow it altogether. What did it *really* mean?"

Stanley, who never followed any poem, was more than a little annoyed that Miss McGoffin should have interrupted him at this moment when his mind was full of plans for the new swimming-pool which he had contracted to build. Without turning to scrutinise her, and thinking her Nordic silhouette as false as his own, he attempted to interpret the poem to which he had not been listening.

"Taken in a nutshell, it means that niggers have a hell of a time in this God-damned country. That's all Negro poets write about."

"Oh!" There was so much abject and unsimulated consternation in Miss McGoffin's cry that Stanley was instantly aware of his mistake.

"I beg your pardon, madam," he pleaded, "but if you will analyze that sentence, you will see that I was neither swearing nor blaspheming, but merely stating a fact."

But the outraged missionary lady had already swept away in what is commonly known as high dudgeon.

"That's a very rude young man over there," she complained to Constancia.

"Which one?" Constancia was prepared to see any one of her guests pointed out to her.

"That *white* one, I blush to say," deplored Miss McGoffin, pointing to Stanley, who was drowning his chagrin in another cocktail.

"Oh," laughed Constancia; and she was just about to explain to Miss McGoffin that Stanley was not as Nordic as he appeared, when Lottie Smith, who adored Stanley, pulled her away.

"Don't enlighten her," Lottie implored. "So long as she thinks Stanley belongs on *her* side of the fence, let her. She might have him lynched!"

It was at this juncture that Constancia, hearing herself asked for in tones which indicated that the quester still had her acquaintance to make, turned to greet a tall, thin-lipped man whose extreme pallor gave him a funereal and apocryphal look.

He was somberly attired in a suit of thick black material the ancient cut of which imparted to the onlookers that thrill which some natives always experience in anything which can be labeled foreign, whether it be a lack of good manners, or the apparent resolution to dress as unlike one's fellowmen as possible.

"Professor Calhoun, I opine?" asked Constancia, coming up to him and extending a brilliant-covered, ivory-pale hand which the professor chose to ignore as he bowed in a formally stiff and embarrassed manner.

"I am afraid there has been some mistake." He drawled the words in a tone with which phonetics can never cope, but there was in it all the laziness and languor which evoke a panorama of cotton-fields, red-clay earth, bandanna handkerchiefs, and Negro women suckling at their breasts white infants whose claim to distinction and aristocracy when they are older will be the fact that they milked those somber breasts.

"If there has been an error, it has been one of omission rather than of commission," confessed Constancia. "In engaging you through your lecture bureau, I did not deem it necessary to indicate my racial handicap. I feared you might be shy about lecturing before people on whom, from what I have read of your discourses, you have such

valuable and esoteric information. I am prepared
to pay the honorarium exacted by your bureau; I
hope you are prepared to fill your part of the con-
tract."

She spoke and looked as if she felt that there
could be no doubt that the professor would fulfill
his part of the mysterious bargain; nevertheless, in
both her speech and her regard there was a trace
of mockery and a challenge, which the professor
chose to accept.

"I am prepared to fulfill my part of the con-
tract, madam, but not to deviate from the usual
tone and procedure of my lectures," he replied,
pursing his lips dryly.

"That is more than satisfactory to me," said
Constancia, with a smile. "In my home you are in
a veritable temple whose reigning deity is free
speech; if I stooped to facetiousness I might even
say of unbridled loquacity. I should feel that I had
been cheated should I have the impression, after
your lecture, that you had altered or suppressed
one thought out of deference for or courtesy to
your audience. And as your hostess, I am willing
to answer for your safety."

As she led her gangling guest across the room
she smiled to herself, as the gods must smile just
when they are about to let loose upon the earth
some plague, or some divine prank like a cyclone

or a tornado, which mortals must submit to, good grace or bad. She felt as if she were making history, as indeed she was.

It is said that in some rural districts where calendars are not as prevalent as sun and rain and death, and where the days glide by without any very definite way existing of marking them, the denizens of those regions have quaint but adequate means of referring to the past. "That happened," they will tell you, "the year John's heifer had her brindled calf," or "Sue was born the year lightning struck her mother's apple tree." And quaint as these temporal devices may appear to those who are calendar born, they probably evoke more intensive responses in the listeners than the recital of a mere number might do. Even so, there are still persons in Harlem who designate the happenings of a certain year as having taken place "the year the Southern professor lectured at Constancia Brandon's." A Harlem journal recapitulating in its column of "today's events, one, five, or ten years ago," will never omit, when the anniversary rolls around, to remind its readers that "today this many years ago, Professor Seth Calhoun of Alabama lectured at the home of Mrs. Constancia Brandon."

A genius for the unusual, coupled with a desire to maintain at any cost the high standard of amusement and instruction which she had set for herself as being indispensable to the success of her *soirées*, had caused Constancia to engage Professor Calhoun to lecture before the Booklovers' Society. The decision called for a temerity bordering on both the cruel and the ridiculous at the same time; but those questions of propriety and suitability which another hostess might have been obliged to ponder long and seriously were airily dismissed by Constancia. The idea intrigued her; it would be the acid test to which she would submit the hordes of guests who drank her wine, danced away the shining surface of her floors, and kept her house in that continual state of happy disorder which was really dear to her heart. This would be a means of separating the sheep from the goats, and of discovering if the Negro really had the sense of humor which some people attributed to him.

"An irrefutable evidence of a sense of humor," she thought, "is the ability to laugh at oneself, as well as at one's tormentors and defamers. If we haven't learned that in these three hundred years, we have made sorry progress."

And she had invited her professor.

Professor Calhoun until that winter had been an obscure teacher of sociology in an even more obscure Southern college. But during all his lean and undistinguished years he had been writing a book which had finally appeared under the title of *The Menace of the Negro to Our American Civilization*. The tract had been composed with a bitterness and a fierceness that had aroused the country to the dark peril which confronted it. Lynchings doubled, the professor's own state leading in gracious compliment to its scribe; mothers kept their children in after dark, while many a gay and debonair young blood was informed in no uncertain terms that he would immediately be cut off without a penny were it discovered that he had been philandering with a maiden not strictly Anglo-Saxon. The women's clubs and the Rotary associations of all the larger American cities invited the professor to come, for magnificent fees, to explain further the growth of this horrible cancer which had at first been but a negligible scratch on the national anatomy. The lectures, to be sure, were but a repetition of the contents of the book, but there was the added attraction of beholding the crusader in his glory. Constancia had paid three dollars and eighty-five cents to hear him lecture at one of the city auditoriums. Unless one scrutinized her closely, her cream-colored face gave little indication that she belonged to the American pariahs; and she had sat serenely through the professor's lecture, fascinated and amused, hearing herself and those of her ilk called in language which was at once musical, courtly, and vituperative, everything except a child of God.

Now as she led the famished-seeming lecturer to a corner of the room where she had already provided a pitcher of water and a glass set on a table on which he might lean should he become nervous, she had her first feeling of apprehension. She wondered if her guests were as intelligent as she hoped they would be, if they would crown her effrontery with success or let her down in ignominious defeat. She was not reassured by hearing Bradley Norris whisper to Stanley Bickford, just as she and Professor Calhoun passed by, "It must be Ichabod Crane." But she shook her head just a trifle more gayly and stepped just a bit more jauntily as she walked past them. She motioned the professor to a chair, and then braced herself firmly against the side of the table in preparation for a speech on which more depended than on any speech which she had ever made.

"Friends and members of the Booklovers' Society"—her voice was tinged with the slightest tremolo, her gray eyes were wide in a way which was evidence of the seriousness of what she was about to say—"it has been many a day since we have had the I hope not dubious distinction of being addressed by a personage as sought-after, and as much in the public eye and on the tip of the public tongue, as our guest of the evening. I think it was the mellow bard of Scotland who importuned Heaven for the insight into himself that he might scrutinize his ego as others beheld it. We are going to be granted a poet's prayer this evening; we are to see ourselves as by one who has studied us long and ardently, with a microscopic seriousness that has revealed some things to him which our simple mirrors have been reticent about revealing to us. As your hostess and his, I have pledged him your discreet and impartial attention. You have no idea what *sort* of pleasure it affords me to introduce to you Professor Seth Calhoun, who will address us on "The Menace of the Negro to Our American Civilization."

Like a bit of willow waving in the wind she turned to the professor, and clapped her fine and tapering hands together. For a moment that seemed an eternity to her there was silence in the room, and then her guests showed their mettle. Their applause invaded and gladdened the heart of their hostess; the professor rose to speak before an audience whose acclamation eclipsed that of any before which he had ever spoken. Since there was not a person there who had not heard of him and who was not aware of his thoughts on his particular subject, the applause was more for Constancia's boldness than for any pleasure which they hoped to experience from what they were about to hear. There were, however, three renegades in the room who could not bring themselves to see the humor of the situation, three who sat with hands tightly clasped in a futile spiritual agony. Miss McGoffin had not forgiven Stanley Bickford's interpretation of Bradley Norris' poem; now hearing the professor's name called, she was forced to clutch the rounds of her chair and to bite down savagely on a bloodless lip lest she make herself ridiculous and add to the further confusion of this strange evening by fainting. She heartily wished she were anywhere at all at the moment save in Constancia's drawing-room. Every delicate fiber in her frail, missionary-abolitionist frame tingled with horror. Surely, she felt, the world was topsy-turvy and everybody in it madder than Alice's hatter, when a person like Professor Seth Calhoun could accept an invitation to speak at the home of a Mrs. Constancia Brandon. As for Donald Hewitt, his gentle English spirit was aroused to battle. He was all for rising and booting the professor into outer darkness, and might have utterly ruined himself in Constancia's eyes had Walter Derwent not held him back.

"But she can't know the man," Donald protested. "She can't have an idea of what he is apt to say, or she would never have invited him."

"Oh yes, she has," said Walter, still firmly holding on to Donald's coat. "No one is going to enjoy this half as much as Constancia, not even the professor."

Donald sank back with a sigh of resignation and distress.

Mrs. De Peyster Johnson, feeling that the columns of the temple which she had erected to the New Negro were about to tumble about her ears, rose to leave, intent on taking her lares and penates with her while they were yet intact. Unfortunately, she had to pass by Constancia, who grasped her firmly by the arm, pulled her down to a chair beside her and directly facing the professor, whispering at the same time, "If you desert me in this my hour of need, there can be no subsequent parley on reparations."

Whatever else the professor may have been, and however much he may have deserved the application of certain uncomplimentary epithets masquerading behind the serene brows of his auditors, it can in no wise be said of him that he was cowardly. The Douglas in his hall frightened him not a bit. Some have said that his hands shook slightly as he held his typewritten manuscript before him, and that under cover of the thick walnut table his knees had a tendency to meet; but Constancia, who was nearest him, avowed that he was the soul of precision and coolness.

"Frigider than a cucumber," she always said whenever she related the incident.

For well beyond an hour he stood before them, and in a warm Southern tone, which was none the less decided, told them about themselves; while Miss McGoffin with each successive point prayed that the floor might open up and engulf her; while Donald Hewitt sat miserably holding a hand tightly over his eyes, as was his childish way when spiritually disturbed; while Walter Derwent sat in a corner and took notes, already shaping in his mind some clever sentence which he would employ in his recital of the affair; while Mrs. De Peyster Johnson became more and more the picture of race-consciousness outraged and trampled upon; while Constancia sat at the professor's side and fanned herself placidly with a green ostrich feather; while the rest of the audience, for the most part, sat in respectful silence. The professor's voice gained in strength and conviction as he mounted toward his peroration. From time to time, Stanley Bickford would applaud at some particularly telling denunciation of Negro morals and manners. These were the moments when Miss McGoffin most wished that she were not present; for while it was intensely unpleasant that one white man should stand before these poor people, and thus injure them, it was even more disturbing that another representative of her race (as she imagined Stanley to be) should add insult to injury by such gratuitous approval.

"It cannot be denied by a person of refined sensibilities that the Negro generally exudes a most unpleasant and disagreeable odor." It is to be noted that the professor had some difficulty with the word Negro; his acquaintance with the term seemed to be of recent date, for it cannot be said that his pronunciation of it was of the clearest; he pronounced it somewhat as a cross between *negro* and *nigra*, as if making a concession to both a momentary courtesy and to custom.

"Hear! Hear!" cried Stanley Bickford as the professor demonstrated the ineffectuality of soaps, unguents, and perfumes against the native odor of the Negro.

"How very discouraging," complained Lottie Smith to Stanley Bickford. "Here I am sprinkled down with *quelques fleurs*, and what's the use?"

Bradley Norris had a nasty and mischievous thought running through his head. He wondered if the potency of the racial odor was in direct proportion to the lack of Caucasian admixture. If so, he marveled how the professor could remain in the same room with Mrs. De Peyster Johnson.

And if the Duchess of Uganda should arrive, they would all be obliged to clear out!

The professor's summary was a gem. The many-colored coat of all the fanatics and zealots of all time seemed to descend upon and envelop him, as with shining eyes he declared in senatorial tones, "It is the duty of white America to look to itself, to protect its sons and daughters from the insidious and growing infiltration of black blood into the arteries of this glorious Republic. There can be no quarter between the white man and a race which can truthfully be stigmatized as indolent, untrustworthy, unintelligent, unclean, immoral, and cursed of heaven. Their only salvation and ours lies in a congressional enactment returning them to Africa, the land of their fathers."

The Duchess of Uganda and Lady Hyacinth Brown, who had been attending a meeting of the Back-to-Africa movement earlier in the evening, and who had arrived in time to hear just the closing portion of the professor's lecture, led the applause which shook the house as the professor sat down. Whatever else he may have said, his ideas about Africa were in accord with those of the duchess and of Lady Hyacinth. The professor sat flushed and uncomfortable, now that his speech was over, while the applause augmented instead of subsiding. Constancia, turning toward Mrs. De

Peyster Johnson, was shocked to find that race-conscious lady sitting with her hands tightly pressed, lest they indulge in approbation against her will.

"Why, Mrs. De Peyster Johnson," protested Constancia, "have you no sense of appreciation? Do applaud, if you don't want to mortify me completely."

"Is it *compulsory*, Constancia?" The racial indignation in Mrs. De Peyster Johnson's voice would have melted a heart of stone, but not Constancia's.

"It's the very framework of the temple," she said, so firmly that Mrs. De Peyster Johnson was prevailed upon to bring her hands together in two quick pats which were as loud as the brushing of two feathers against one another. However, the gesture was enough to placate Constancia.

Lecturers and speakers were never submitted to the grueling of a questioning period at Constancia's. It was her conviction that if they had not been able to impart their ideas to their audience during the hour allotted them, they were probably undecided themselves as to just what their thoughts were. In the case of Professor Calhoun there could be no doubt as to what his thoughts were on the Negro.

The Duchess of Uganda, with her beautiful

soot-black face, like that of a Botticelli cherub, in shocking contrast with her huge shapeless body, had hemmed the professor in.

"I cannot say that I had the pleasure of hearing the whole of your discourse, which, if it was on a par with the ending, must have been very inspiring," the duchess was saying in a voice which was really beautiful and which Constancia always spoke of as being "so divinely contrastful to the duchess' body," "but I am in hearty agreement with your ideas on the rehabilitation of Africa by the American Negro. Oh, the green forests of Africa, the amber water of the Nile, the undiscovered oases of the Sahara, what foundations to build upon!"

"The duchess is an elocutionist by *métier*," explained Constancia to the slightly alarmed professor. "Won't you let me offer you something after your strenuous discourse, something by way of refreshment, a glass of punch perhaps?"

Reaching forward to take from a tray which Porter was carrying a thin glass of scarlet iced liquid, she smiled as she noticed the professor's hesitation and embarrassment.

"Maybe you are thinking of running for political office somewhere in your part of the country, professor, or of lecturing in some of the larger Southern cities, and it would not be distinctly to

your advantage if the news of this evening's condescension reached those sections. I promise you that
the papers will carry nothing of it, and that your
constituents will be left in blissful ignorance of
your courtesy." She held the glass out temptingly
toward him.

The professor smiled in spite of himself. "This
will be my first time, madam," he explained, as he
took the glass, "to eat or drink with Negroes."

"Really, Professor?" asked Constancia as she
clinked glasses with him. "Do you mean to tell me
that this is your first time to have social intercourse
with Negroes?"

"My first, madam," reiterated the professor,
gravely.

"Ah"—Constancia waggled her finger at him—
"you are indeed tardy in arriving at what your section of the country has been doing for years."

The professor had drained his glass. He stood
awkwardly, turning it in his hand.

"Allow me," said Constancia as she extended
her hand to relieve him of the toy. Then, as he
passed the glass to her, and just as it appeared to
be safely within her grasp, she allowed it, inadvertently—ah, certainly inadvertently—to fall to
the floor, where it splintered on the hearth. Her
sparkling eyes met the professor's unflinchingly.
"*Mea culpa*, Professor," she sighed, adding, "I am

sure you must be fatigued by now and longing to get away." She reached down into a bosom fragrant with powder and perfume, and perhaps with those odors which the professor had so deplored. Her eyes twinkled as she handed him an envelope. "Here is your fee, Professor, and thank you for a pleasant and instructive evening."

"A bull's-eye!" whispered Walter Derwent to Donald as he wildly scribbled the scene on the back of an envelope.

In spite of the enthusiastic reception accorded it, the professor's lecture seemed to have dampened the usual high spirits which prevailed at these meetings. Constancia's guests left early, apparently in need of repose after having seen themselves through the professor's lens. Donald Hewitt was the last to depart. He loitered around until only he, George, and Constancia remained. Then it was that he took his hostess' hand and kissed it fervently, too young and naïve to veil his ardor because of George's presence.

"Madam," said the young Englishman, "you are lovely, you are marvelous! I adore you!"

Constancia had an intuitive feeling that this was one of the most genuine speeches Donald had ever made.

She let her fingers stray lightly over the blond

head still bent above her hand. "How old are you?" she asked, gently.

"Twenty-two." Donald proclaimed it proudly as if it were the year of wisdom and of love.

"And I am on the other side of thirty-five," said Constancia. "There is just enough similarity in our ages for us to be very good friends. Good night. And come whenever you want to again. I give you *carte blanche.*"

"George," she cajoled, as with her husband's arm around her waist she slowly climbed the stairs to their bedroom, "you must learn to kiss my hand like that young Englishman. It means much to a woman on the other side of thirty-five."

Chapter Ten

WHEN Constancia had hit upon the kind and generous impulse of marrying Mattie from her home, she had had no ulterior motive in view, had envisaged no future date when Sam would add to her popularity and prestige by contributing to the success of one of her evenings, even though at the expense of the Duchess of Uganda. But Constancia had been born under a lucky star and belonged to that fortunate group to whom, having much, the heavens with inexplicable and illogical generosity promise more.

That a wedding may be a matter of great momentary importance, yet not magical enough to change the ingrained thoughts and actions of a lifetime in the twinkling of an eye, Mattie was to learn slowly and sorrowfully in her fitful experience with Sam. When he asked her to marry him, he had done so only after what to him was due deliberation, and with the wavering intention that surely he would find work to do the next day or the next week after his marriage. It was, however, fully two months after, and then only due to Con-

stancia's intervention, that he drew in his long
legs from in front of the parlor stove and set out
to earn his share of his and Mattie's living.

Mattie had been too deep in love and too lost
in religion to scold, or to show by word or look
that she was hurt or disappointed. With her religion had come a fatalism, and she was leaving all
to the Lord. Daily Aunt Mandy nagged her for
keeping a good-for-nothing man lying around the
house and in her way, although daily the old lady
took out her cards, read Sam's fortune, and then
became his partner in one of the many card games
he had taught her. Daily Mattie was forced to answer in the negative when Constancia asked if
Sam had started to work. Finally Constancia had
taken the matter in hand herself, and with Mattie
at her side had routed Sam away from the fire one
March morning, and had taken him to a job. It
was a job with a uniform, much to Aunt Mandy's
joy, and with great prestige and privilege attached,
although the nature of it was not entirely to Mattie's liking. It savored too much of the world, the
flesh, and the devil. Constancia had been able to
do nothing better than to secure Sam the rôle of
ticket-chopper in one of the small variety and
movie houses of the neighborhood. It was work
which could be manipulated with one hand, and
which at the same time, with the attendant uni-

form, afforded Sam a real opportunity to show off
his fine height and slim, swaggering figure.

It was a gorgeous uniform of smooth bright
green material, with square padded shoulders,
gold epaulettes, and with black braid fronting the
sleeves and surrounding the buttonholes through
which large brass buttons shot their fire. Sam felt
like a general or drum-major, and thought that
working might not be so distasteful as long as he
could be attired in such a manner.

The evening on which he first donned his glory
happened to be one on which Mattie had been retained at Constancia's, where a party was being
given for Herbert Newell, a young Negro who had
just published a novel. As the doors of the theater
swung open to liberate its audience from the land
of fancy and at the same time to liberate Sam from
his toil, he thought it might be a pleasant idea if
he passed by Constancia's in order to wait for
Mattie and to walk home with her, and inciden-
tally to let her feast her eyes upon his new-spun
raiment. Unfortunately, he liked himself so well
in his new finery that he thought it worthy of a
stimulant, with the result that by the time he
reached Constancia's home it was only by the
bright lights which illumined the house from roof
to cellar, and by that second sense which some

drunken men seem to acquire, that he was able to locate his destination.

The party was for Herbert Newell, but the evening became that of the duchess and of Sam. Not many people had read Herbert's novel, although it had been out for several months and had been commented upon in the Negro and white press (denounced by the former as an outrage against Negro sensibilities, and lauded by the latter as being typically Negro), yet almost everyone present came up to the author, shook his hand, and congratulated him. Poor outspoken Lottie Smith naïvely made herself an enemy for life by admitting that she was waiting to borrow Constancia's copy of the new book. Herbert, a very dark, belligerent young Negro, was brutally frank, and shocked several of the more sentimentally minded guests by informing them that art as such didn't mean anything to him, and that he had not written his book for the sake of anything so nebulous, but merely to make some money.

"Not," he added, "that I expect to make it from Negroes."

"I suppose I shall buy it," sighed Mrs. Vanderbilt-Jones in a tone of deep resignation. "I'll buy it out of pride of race, although from what I hear, I shall hardly like it, I fear. I don't see why our writers don't write about *nice* people sometimes."

She gazed grandiloquently around the room to show Herbert the fine material at hand.

"Yes, Herbert," interposed Constancia, who had just come up at this point. "I understand that the heroine of your book is a prostitute, and that the hero is a stevedore. How can anything good come out of Nazareth, or anything to which we as a race can point to with pride come out of a combination like that? I quite agree with Mrs. Vanderbilt-Jones. You should have written about people like Counselor Spivens, who has just been incarcerated for a year for converting to his own use money awarded one of his clients in an equal-rights case; or like Dr. Strong, whose new limousine is the reward of Heavens knows how many abortions; or you might have woven a highly colorful tale around Mrs. Vanderbilt-Jones' own niece, Betty, who just . . ."

"Constancia," interrupted the old lady as she flounced off, "if I didn't love you so much I should positively hate you."

Constancia smiled and laid her hand on Herbert's arm. "Write whatever you want, Herbert, and don't give a continental about them. It will take them centuries, anyway, to distinguish between good and bad, and what is nice and what is really smeared over with a coating which they call nice. I just heard poor Mrs. De Peyster Johnson, to whose credit it can at least be said that she has read your book, declare, simply because you are a New Negro and therefore dear to her heart, that your novel was as good as anything that Wells or Bennett had written. And when I added that it was much better than anything written by any of the Russians, she agreed heartily. That's race pride with a vengeance for you, and self-criticism that isn't worth a penny."

"I wish they were all like you, Constancia," Herbert assured her. "I'd know then that they had some intelligence, and that when they condemned my book they had something to back up their dislike, and that when they said they liked it they were really doing something more sincere than making conversation with me. Half a dozen of them tonight have already asked me what the white people will think about the race when they read my book. Good God! I wasn't writing a history about the Negro. I was trying to write a novel."

"Yes," agreed Constancia as she waved to the duchess and to Lady Hyacinth Brown, who had just come in, "I suppose there are any number of us who pass perfectly wretched nights sleeping on our backs instead of on our stomachs, which we would find more comfortable, because we fear

what the white world might say about the Negro
race."

"Sometimes it makes me feel like I should like
to chuck it and pass for something else," said Herbert, seriously, although a near-by glass which gave
back his countenance showed one which was far
too sable to pass as anything Caucasian, not even
excepting the Italian and the Spanish.

"I never feel like that," said Constancia. "God
knows there is nothing chauvinistic about me. I
often think the Negro is God Almighty's one mistake, but as I look about me at white people, I am
forced to say so are we all. It isn't being colored
that annoys me. I could go white if I wanted to,
but I am too much of a hedonist; I enjoy life too
much, and enjoyment isn't across the line. Money
is there, and privilege, and the sort of power which
comes with numbers; but as for enjoyment, they
don't know what it is. When I go to so-called white
parties sometimes and look around me, I have a
feeling that the host has been very wise in break-
ing down color conventions, and that in most
cases his reason is selfish instead of being due to
an interracial complex. I have seen two Negroes
turn more than one dull party, where I was longing for home and Harlem, into a revel which Puck
himself would find it hard to duplicate. As for
variety, I think I should die if I were obliged to

look into the mirror daily and to see nothing but my own parchment-colored skin, or to turn and behold nothing but George's brown visage shining back at me all day long, no matter how much adoration it reflected. When I get tired of George and myself I have simply to phone for Stanley Bickford—and Greenland's icy mountains couldn't send me anything more Nordic, with a nose more aquiline, with more cerulean eyes, or with hair one bit more prickly and blond. Let me dial another number and I have the Duchess of Uganda, black as the ace of spades and more beautiful than Lucifer, or Lottie Smith, brown as a berry and with more real vivacity than a twirling dervish. No, thanks, I wouldn't change. So long as I have my happiness to consider, I'll not go to the mountain. If the mountain wants me, let it come to me. It knows where I am."

"I am going to write a book about you some day, Constancia," threatened Herbert.

"If you call it *Nice People*, it will be a terrible misnomer," said Constancia, turning to greet the duchess and Lady Hyacinth Brown, who were rushing over to their hostess in concerted excitement, if the floating undulation of Lady Hyacinth, a mode of ambulance which she never abandoned even in her most tense moments, and the waddling propulsion of the duchess may be termed rushing.

Behind them like a lost shadow stalked Donald Hewitt.

Some day Lady Hyacinth and the duchess, the latter more deservedly, will find a chronicler worthy of recounting their adventures and of properly fixing their status in Harlem society. They were an excellent foil to one another; yet each was so much the other's complement that since the inception of the Back-to-Africa movement, and since the laying of the accolade upon them, they had been inseparable companions, both working for the same cause, each respecting the power of the other, and neither in the least jealous of her sister's attainments.

By way of explaining the duchess and Lady Hyacinth, it may be noted that the Back-to-Africa movement was the heart and entrails of a society whose aim it was to oppose to the American slogan of "The United States for the White Man" the equally non-inclusive shibboleth of "Africa for the Black Man," in this case, the favored descendant of Ham being the American branch. The society held its meetings in a large barn-like building which had once been a church, and certainly one not dedicated to the gods of Africa. Credit must be given the society for realizing the importance of something which most organizations for civic or racial betterment are inclined to ignore, namely

an appeal to the pleasurable instincts of man. With
the Back-to-Africa movement went costumes that
rivaled those of the private guard of the king of
England; parades up and down the broad avenues
of Harlem every Sunday and once or twice during
the week; thunderous orations at the seat of the
cabal; and wild, heady music blared forth by a
specially trained, constantly practicing brass band.
Added to this was the beautifully naïve and romantic way in which the society marched forward
to meet the future. Its members were not doomed,
like the Israelites, to sweat and toil and perish
many in the wilderness before tasting any of the
joys of their Canaan. The Back-to-Africa movement realized that it was simply a matter of constantly lessening time before Africa should be back
in the hands of its rightful sons and daughters;
therefore, in order to speed the zeal of the members, the officers began to parcel out what they
already considered as properly, even if only re-
motely, theirs. Out of deference to the existing
powers they did not proclaim an Emperor of
Africa, but they did elect a President for the
Nonce. With his election their deference to lesser
dignitaries ceased, and the far-off, unsuspecting
African territories were parceled out left and
right, as dukes, counts, and marquises of Africa
were created without stint and without thought of

the complications which might arise should the Negroes, once returned to their ancestral home, decide upon a republican form of government.

It had been a bright day indeed for her who had been born simple Mary Johnson (as she was often reminded by Constancia when the spirit of the malicious was upon her) when the President for the Nonce of the African Empire, in recognition of fifteen thousand dollars which her argumentative talents had garnered for the general coffers of the society, had bidden her kneel, had laid his accolade upon her, and then had bidden her rise, Mary Johnson no longer, but Mary, Duchess of Uganda, first of her line, and spiritual and temporal head of the house of Uganda.

It had been a day no less luminous and no less marked of Heaven when she whose husband was a mere government employee, too stubbornly intrenched in the monthly assurance of a government check to see rising into the future the glorious edifices of the New Africa, had also knelt to rise, in recognition of ten thousand dollars raised for the general coffers, Mrs. Hyacinth Brown no longer, but Lady Hyacinth Brown, undisturbed by the social complications of a mulish husband who must continue to be introduced as plain Mr. Brown.

With their advent into the nobility there came

a rise in social importance if not in actual social status.. Few Harlem hostesses could forbear the pleasurable thrill of including on their guest lists the names of the duchess and of Lady Hyacinth. To be sure, as the wife of a railway mail clerk, Lady Hyacinth had already possessed a not un-enviable niche in Harlem society; whereas the duchess, as a once-talented, if now slightly declin-ing elocutionist, had also been greatly in demand; but the glories of governmental patronage and of elocution were shabby indeed in comparison with those of nobility.

Lady Hyacinth, being the less complicated per-sonage, is the more quickly disposed of. She was a special type from which a well-known and dis-turbing generality has been drawn for almost every play or novel written to combat miscegena-tion. Any young Englishman, colonial expatriate, or Southern aristocrat left unprotected with her for five minutes was certain to develop an in-curable case of *mammy palaver*. Her elongated languorous body, deep-sunken eyes shaded with heavy velvet lashes, the perfect blending of colors in her skin, and her evident consciousness of her seductive powers, would have arrested any author in search of the perfect half-caste siren. The only drawback was that one soon tired of Lady Hya-cinth; she was neither witty, amusing, nor intelligent; she was merely disturbingly beautiful. She was clever enough, however, to ally herself with the duchess and, when the moment presented itself, to shine by silent comparison.

But the duchess was a character, a creation, a personage in whose presence one felt the stir of wings and heavenly vibrations. Constancia declared the duchess was as beautiful as Satan; but she erred; there was nothing Satanic or diabolic about the duchess, not even when she was descanting upon the beauties of that Africa which she had never seen. Indeed, looking at her, one was apt to feel, if he could forget the body to which it was attached, that some divine sculptor had taken a block of the purest black marble and from it had chiseled that classic head. She reminded one of beautiful Queen Niferti. In her youth, when her figure, trim and lissom, was a perfect adjunct to the beauty of her face, the duchess had been the toast of half of Negrodom, including many who until they gazed upon her had never felt that beauty could reside in blackness unadulterated. Now in her fortieth year, only in the shapelessness of that bulk with which the years had weighted her down, did she give evidence of the cruelty of time; her face still retained the imperishable beauty of black marble.

The duchess had come along in a day and time

when the searing flare for the dramatic which gnawed at her entrails had had no dignified outlet. There was little which a black girl, however beautiful, might do on the stage; and because Mary Johnson, even as a girl, had been the soul of dignity, she had put the stage out of her mind as something unattainable, and had decided to be an elocutionist. Even so, the way had been hard and thorny. The duchess was not one to truckle; she certainly had not forsworn the stage in order to lend herself as a diseuse to anything less than dignified, and to little less than might be labeled classic. Therefore to Negro audiences which might have rallied to her support, had she regaled them with the warm dialect of "When Malindy Sings" and "The Party," she chose to interpret scenes from "Macbeth," "Hamlet," and "The Merchant of Venice." To audiences and intelligences to whom it was utterly unimportant whether the quality of mercy was strained or not, she portrayed in a beautiful and haunting voice the aspirations of a dark Lady Macbeth, the rich subtleties of a sable Portia, and the piteous fate of a black Desdemona.

And success had not been hers.

Finally, as many another artist has turned from the dream of his youth to something baser but more remunerative, the duchess, in the face of want, had turned from elocution to dressmaking. Her nimble fingers and inventive mind had done for her what her voice had failed to accomplish; money had rolled in until she had finally been able to open two shops and to do nothing herself save supervise.

But the worm of an unfulfilled ambition lay tightly curled at the root of material success; and at the dropping of a handkerchief the duchess would willingly recite for any club, charity benefit, or simple social gathering.

With the passing of the years she had developed a decided predilection for martial pieces and had added to her standard Shakespearian repertoire such hardly perennials as "I am dying, Egypt, dying," "The Charge of the Light Brigade," and "The Black Regiment." The recital of the gallant doings at Balaclava had once thrown her into a state of embarrassment from which only Constancia's quick wit had saved her. The members of the United Daughters of African Descent still chuckle at the memory of it.

It happened at the annual meeting of the Daughters, a conclave at which Constancia, in the guise of mistress of ceremonies, had finally heeded the duchess' importunings, and had called upon her for a recitation. The duchess was charmed, and she looked to Tennyson's poem to help her to eclipse totally all other participants on the program. She began beautifully, her "Half a league, half a league, half a league onward" soaring over the benches into the gallery of the auditorium and completely terminating every whisper. Never before had the Daughters given such gracious attention. But midway of the glorious account, at what would seem the crucial moment, something went blank in the duchess' mind, or, to be more exact, her memory failed her absolutely. Her right arm was raised, her right foot extended and pointed, as she proclaimed "Cannon to right of them." Twice she repeated the designation of that particular section of cannon. Her memory still in abeyance, she was so discountenanced and flustered at the fourth repetition that even her usual beautiful diction suffered, with the result that she uttered unmistakably, "*Cannern* to right of them." It was then that Constancia, who was seated behind her, pulled the duchess' sleeve, at the same time importuning her in a whisper which escaped no one, "For God's sake, Duchess, genuflex and sit down."

A singular comradeship had sprung up between the duchess and Donald Hewitt, and Harlem soon became accustomed to the sight of the tall, fair-haired, imbibing Englishman, more often tottering than maintaining that dignity which is held synonymous with his nationality, accompanied by the short, hard-breathing, elocutionist. They complemented one another's educations admirably. Into dens and retreats of which she had never dreamed the duchess followed Donald, squeezed her gargantuan form into diminutive chairs, and bravely sipped at strange, fiery beverages while Donald gulped down others by the score. Impervious to the imprecations hurled at them by those with whom they collided, they would often dance everyone else from the floor until they alone were left, free to dip and glide and pirouette from one end of the dance space to the other. Then back at their seats, just as his head began to sag and his eyes to glaze, Donald would lean across the table, plant the blond refractory head firmly on his crossed elbows, and beseech the duchess to recite. It is to be doubted that the melancholy soliloquy of Denmark's prince or the gentle pleadings of Portia have ever been uttered under stranger auspices. Over the savage blare of brass and the shrill screeching of strings, cutting into the thick, sickening closeness of cabaret smoke, drowning the obscene hilarity of amorous women, reprimanding the superimposed bragadoccio of inebriated males, the beautiful voice of the duchess would rise, clear and harmonious, winging across the table to Donald. *"To be or not to be. . . ."*

The pure sweet voice of African nobility would go on soothing one of England's disillusioned children with the divine musings of England's best. *"Nymph, in thy orisons, Be all my sins remembered."* Often as not when the last soft syllable fell from the duchess' lips, England's son would be peacefully sleeping; for always when the duchess began a Shakespearian recitation, Donald was forced to veil his eyes. With the most charming frankness he had explained his reason for this seeming discourtesy to Constancia one evening when she came upon him with covered eyes while the duchess, as Ophelia, was declaiming, *"O heat, dry up my brains! tears seven times salt, Burn out the sense and virtue of mine eye!"*

"I adore the duchess," Donald had apologized, "but I simply cannot look at her when she does Shakespeare. Her voice is as divine as any I have ever heard, but her color and form collide with all my remembered Ophelias and Portias. I cannot get those tall, flaxen-haired women of my race out of my mind; they linger there so obstinately that the duchess, so physically dissimilar, for all the ebony loveliness of her face, looms like a moving blasphemy on the horizon of my memory. But you won't tell her, Constancia, will you?"

Constancia had promised to keep his secret; so Donald continued, whenever it was a question of

the duchess' Shakespearian repertoire, for which
he himself often asked, to shade his eyes, thereby
gaining for himself the reputation of being her
most sincere and enamored admirer.

It was never a question of anything more between them than open and candid comradeship;
they amused one another, and life seemed more
pleasant to them because of the acquaintance.
Such a mild state of affairs irked Lady Hyacinth,
who looked upon Donald with a favorably prejudiced eye which, alas! found no answering gleam
in those blue orbs so childishly centered upon the
duchess.

It was give and take between Donald and the
duchess. If he dragged her off nightly to mush-
room-growth cabarets, or insisted upon taking her
to Park Avenue teas where she was lorgnetted and
avoided by all except her constant companion and
a few daring males, she also had her hour. Docilely
Donald followed her to Back-to-Africa meetings,
where he sat, hot and uncomfortable, beneath the
hostile gaze of thousands for whom he was but another inquisitive and undesired representative of
all that was bleached and base; and it was only the
duchess' extended scepter that secured him grace
and safety. The duchess piloted him in and out of
dark, mysterious hallways, made him climb innumerable flights of creaking stairs as she went her

rounds soliciting funds for the movement. Never did he balk, for always he envisioned the evening's close—music, dancing, the slow fumes from forbidden beverages insinuating their wily passage into his brain, and across the table from him a beautiful black, middle-aged sybil ready to lull him to sleep with the opium of the world's dramatic wisdom.

Constancia, although ordinarily charity itself, had no sympathy with the duchess' nostalgia for Africa, and had never opened her purse to the duchess' insistent and plaintive pleadings for a donation to the cause. "I am in favor of back-to-nature movements," she excused herself, "for everybody except George and myself. George knows nothing about African diseases, and I can't abide tsetse flies, tarantulas, and dresses made out of grass. No, thank you, I wouldn't change Seventh Avenue for the broadest boulevard along the Congo."

"You are totally devoid of race pride, Constancia," the duchess had complained, bitterly, an indictment against which Constancia knew it was useless to defend herself.

Donald, equally unsympathetic to the Back-to-Africa movement, and marveling how any inhabitant of Harlem could look forward with relish to life in Africa, had been less impervious to his comrade's entreaties. He had capitulated by giving the duchess a princely check, accompanied by the ungentlemanly and unphilanthropic wish that it might do the movement no good whatever, and that, should it ever be used toward the purchase of a ship, that unholy conveyance might get no further than New York Harbor.

The reason for the duchess' and Lady Hyacinth's excitement the night of the party for Herbert Newell was soon made apparent. Both the noble ladies were panting with an unsimulated eagerness to be the first to break the important news, but Donald, who was ironically calm, if a bit unsteady, stole their thunder.

"The duchess has just discovered a marvelous record concerning the aviatic exploits of one Lieutenant Julian," he explained. "A marvelous poem, set to entrancing, barbaric music. The noble sentiments expressed in the verses make the duchess and Lady Hyacinth certain that the record can be a mighty weapon in awakening the American Negro to a sense of his duty. In order to aid the duchess in a work with which I have not the slightest sympathy, I have just donated one hundred of these records to the cause. The duchess contemplates sending them to all the centers where there are branches of the Back-to-Africa movement. I've brought along one for you to listen to."

They had to crowd close to the victrola in order to hear; for near by Mrs. Vanderbilt-Jones and Agatha Winston, a sleek, *café-au-lait* soubrette, who had just returned from eighteen months of European triumphs, were having a shouting bout. Agatha had gone to London over three years past with a sepia-colored musical comedy which had not caused a conflagration on the Thames. The sponsor of the engagement had paid the actors a tithe of the wages promised them, and then had left them to scuttle for themselves. And they had scuttled in dreary, dejected bands of three and four, some back to America, others across Europe as far as Russia, improvising as they went. An egoistic streak had caused Agatha to shun all offers of partnership, and to shift for herself. She had worked her way to Paris, where a slight ability to sing and dance, the knack of crossing her eyes, and of twisting her limbs out of joint, while attired in the minimum amount of clothes permitted by the French penal code, had soon made her the darling of France. She was now back in America for a brief visit to Harlem, intent on dazzling a world too immersed in having a good time to be more than faintly amused by a French maid, the display of divers gifts from infatuated European royalty, and the consciousness that it all emanated from a talent which could be duplicated and eclipsed in any Harlem pleasure cave.

"An Earl with a coat of mail and everything, and I turned him down," Agatha's voice soared in strident self-approval over the soft preparatory grating of the needle.

"And to think you could have been an earless, the first colored earless in the world, a steppingstone for the race," Mrs. Vanderbilt-Jones shouted back her disapproval, and clucked her tongue.

Clustered around the victrola, Constancia, the duchess, Lady Hyacinth, and Donald formed a trembling and excited group which was soon augmented by Lottie Smith, who, never having been to Europe, couldn't abide Agatha's airs. As the first bars of the rich mongrel music, in which notes of Africa, Harlem, and the Orient could be traced, flooded the room, Lottie rolled her eyes upward in an ecstatic convulsion, and snapped her fingers rhythmically, while the duchess stood with bowed and pensive head, as if the strains of a Negro "Marseillaise" were causing her ample bosom to seethe and stir with patriotism. In gusty Jamaican pride the voice of the singer heralded the exploits of Lieutenant Julian:

> "At last, at last, it has come to pass,
>   *Hélas, hélas!* Lieutenant Julian will fly at last,
>   Lindbergh flew over the sea,
>   Chamberlin flew to Germany,
>   Julian said Paris or eternity."

The chorus with which this melodic eulogy opened set the keynote of racial pride and hope which was to run through the amazing verses:

> "Negroes everywhere,
>   Negroes in this hemisphere,
>   Come, come in a crowd,
>   Come let us all be proud,
>   When he conquers the wave and air,
>   In his glory we are going to share.
>   He said Paris or eternity.
>
> "White men have no fear,
>   White men have conquered the air,
>   Julian with him will compare,
>   About his life he has no fear,
>   Why should we not do what we can
>   To help this brave colored man.
>   He said Paris or eternity."

"They simply *cannot* love like *colored* men," Agatha's indecent and compromising avowal shocked in midair with the termination of the panegyric on Lieutenant Julian.

The duchess heaved a mammoth sigh, and wiped away a pearly tear as the last heroic strains died off.

"What do you think of it?" she asked Constancia, who had not yet recovered.

"Very soulful, Duchess," Constancia assured her.

"And its possibilities?" persisted the duchess.

"Limitless," conceded Constancia.

"I love the change from alas to *hélas* in the chorus," said Lady Hyacinth, dreamily. "I don't know why, but it gives me a catch in my throat, probably because it's so foreign and unexpected."

"I don't think it's so hot as sense," confessed Lottie, bluntly, "but the music would make a grand stomp; it's so aboriginal."

"I am going to use it on the lecture platform," said the duchess, "as I go from city to city addressing our branches. It will inspire thousands to a sense of the possibilities inherent in the simplest black man. I do wish, however, that he had said *Africa* or eternity instead of *Paris*. That would be so much more effective for my purpose."

"Lottie," urged Constancia, anxious to sidetrack the duchess from her favorite topic of African redemption, "won't you sing something for us, the 'St. Louis Blues,' perhaps?"

"There's nobody to play for me," demurred Lottie, "or I would. Stanley's not here yet."

"You might sing '*A Capella*,'" suggested Constancia.

"I'm sorry, Constancia," said Lottie. "You know you never have to beg me, but I don't know '*A Capella*'; and there's nobody to play it, if I did. Maybe the duchess will recite. I love to hear her do that piece where she goes mad and talks so crazy."

"I suppose she means Ophelia," said the duchess, haughtily, ignoring Lottie and addressing herself to Constancia.

"Yes," confessed Lottie, unabashed, "that's the one. I think it's *simply* a scream."

"I assure you that it wasn't written as a scream, Miss Smith"—the duchess' dark eyes were charged with enough indignation and disgust to annihilate a less imperturbable soul than Lottie.

"Have it your own way, Duchess," Lottie retorted, but it's a scream to me."

The duchess did not stoop to further argument, fearful lest an extended discussion rob her of this opportunity to shine.

"I don't feel very Shakespearian tonight," she confided to Constancia. "I feel martial. I feel the urge to recount the heroic doings of my people. I could do either 'Black Samson of Brandywine' or 'The Black Regiment.' Which shall it be?"

"Why not do both, Duchess?" asked Donald, gallantly.

"You dear greedy boy, I will," the duchess conceded as she tousled his hair and inwardly thanked him from the bottom of her heart for affording her an excuse to render both recitations. "I shall start with 'The Black Regiment.' But I must have silence."

She stepped to the center of the floor, where, after bowing profoundly, she stood in meditative and dignified reproval until all the diminutive whispers, sudden coughs, and epileptic squirmings had ceased.

O black heroic regiment whose bravery has been recounted so nobly by the poet Boker, your immortality is assured so long as there remains a Negro elocutionist to chant your glory! From your dust may flowers rise as garlands for the head of the duchess and all her kind! Well might Ethiopia's estranged children, captives in a hostile land, let roll down their gay painted cheeks, a few furtive tears, as the duchess, trembling with pride and devotion, unleashed that divine voice:

"Dark as the clouds of even,
Banked in the western heaven,
Waiting the breath that lifts
All the dread mass, and drifts
Tempest and falling brand,
Over a ruined land—
So still and orderly
Arm to arm, and knee to knee

> Waiting the great event,
> Stands the Black Regiment.

> "Down the long dusky line
>   Teeth gleam and eyeballs shine;
>   And the bright bayonet,
>   Bristling and firmly set,
>   Flashed with a purpose grand
>   Long ere the sharp command
>   Of the fierce rolling drum
>   Told them their time had come—
>   Told them what work was sent
> For the Black Regiment."

There was no need for Donald to veil his eyes now. The duchess was in her element. As if the ghostly regiment stood behind her listening in serried ranks of impalpability to the recital of their bravery, her voice now soft and tender, now rich with frenzy, now high and courageous as if in the midst of battle, swept everything before her. Listening to her, her auditors felt that there was nothing in heaven and hell which their race might not surmount, and even Constancia felt a hard, unfamiliar tightening of the throat. And then that opulent petition to which the lords of the land would never open their ears brought the poem to its close:

> "Hundreds on hundreds fell;
>   But they are resting well;

Scourges and shackles strong
Never shall do them wrong.
Oh! to the living few,
Soldiers, be just and true!
Hail them as comrades tried;
Fight with them side by side;
Never in field or tent
Scorn the Black Regiment!"

By all that is fine and touching there should have been no applause, there should have been nothing but dark bowed heads, their obeisance hiding proud, glistening eyes. And for a full minute the duchess should have stood there, Ethiopia eloquent, stretching forth her hands for justice and equity in exchange for courage and proven fidelity.

And then while the rumor of great and mighty actions was still with them, while the ghosts of the Black Regiment were yet there, suffused with the memory of their mortal greatness, the duchess should have evoked the towering majesty of "Black Samson of Brandywine," that fierce black scythe of destruction whom a black poet has sung and whom black declaimers keep alive.

But, alas for the serene and somber Spirit which hopes to reign supreme and tranquil at a Negro gathering. Shut laughter and railery out; with cotton in every crevice and keyhole bid them begone, yet will they filter their way back through the shaft of light that steals in under the lowered window-shade!

Even as the duchess, sensing the dramatic opportunities of the moment, made the transition from regiment to lone soldier, cleared her throat, and introduced, "Black Samson of Brandywine" —at that moment even, he who in a bright-green uniform with gold epaulettes had made his dizzy way from glass to glass through a maze of streets to Constancia's home, stood beautifully balancing himself in the doorway. The gold buttons flashed their radiance into the room, and mingled their fire with the amber, unclouded enchantment in Constancia's eyes. Like a lioness defending her young, the duchess turned with open mouth and outraged countenance to confront the intruder, while Lottie Smith rose from her chair, shrieking, "It must be Black Samson himself!"

"No," disagreed the enchanted Constancia, as with one hand she supported the tottering duchess, while with the other she beckoned Sam to abandon his perilous perch on the threshold, for a place among the company, "it's only the Emperor Jones!"

Later, as they walked home through the fine Harlem twilight, Mattie rebuked Sam for having endangered her position by his precipitate and unsolicited entrance into her mistress' home; but in her purse was a crisp new bill of generous denomination and in her ears still echoed the laughter with which Constancia had said: "The duchess and Sam made my *soirée*. As I refuse to donate to the Back-to-Africa movement, I am giving this to Sam. And don't scold him."

Chapter Eleven

APRIL, changeable and undecided, blew now warm and now chill on Harlem. And like children playing a game, Harlem ran in and out, sloughing overcoats today, loitering on street corners, sowing in laughter and rich talk the rumors of spring; tomorrow shivering back into yesterday's discarded mantles, grumbling at the indecent insistence of winter. But gradually the cold subsided, day by day lost ground, as Harlem, in Harlem's way, rushed out to meet the spring. For to others spring may come, may be allowed to come slowly and painfully as if in travail, but Negroes go out to meet the spring, and rip it brutally from the too slowly yielding womb of the earth. The thinnest sliver of sunlight, the most tepid harbinger of a zephyr, the first insolent blade of grass feeling its way through pavement crevices, are heralded with drums and banners, as if all the batteries of August's sun were beating down in burning gold and bronze, as if indeed the year had played a trick on spring, and without transition had gone straight to summer.

In Constancia's neighborhood the procedure is more orderly. They too go out to meet the spring, but, being people of circumstance, doctors, lawyers, teachers, owners of houses, payers of direct taxes, their method is genteel and studied. Constancia, to be sure, if it suited her capricious fancy, might thrust her lovely head out into the air, sniff at it like a happy cur, and cry, "Glory!" if she felt so disposed; but not her neighbors. Their ways were not raucous; they who bear the yoke of gentility must bear it as to the manner born. They dance a minuet with spring, and take no step out of season. There is a studied time for the taking down of the winter curtains; there is the precise moment when measures are taken for flower-boxes which in their appointed time will fringe the windows and line the entrance steps; now one does not put the car into the garage so soon, but allows it to remain just outside in the street, in case after supper it might not be deemed too chilly for a drive through the Park. There is a decent time too for bringing one's chair out on the stoop and sitting there awhile. In Constancia's neighborhood one does not change one's winter clothes precipitately for the habiliments of spring, but one goes slowly through all the nuances of diminishing warmth. One's skin is tender, one's lungs are delicate; April is treacherous, and one safeguards one's health. There is more rapport between Constancia's neighborhood and fashionable Fifth Avenue, than between the latter and that of Sam and Mattie, although Sam and Mattie, too, live on Fifth Avenue.

Where Sam and Mattie live one cannot take time to mince words, one cannot be exact about when winter curtains go up and when they come down. Suddenly you discover that Christmas is within hailing distance; this morning the lady for whom you do day's work had you put up her curtains; and so tonight, though tired, you hang your own. Suddenly it is warm again; you feel spring on your cheek; Mrs. Cohen will not have her curtains down until the 15th of April, but yours go down today. Order and precision are part and parcel of means; they get mislaid in the struggle for existence, as do many other of the niceties which obtain in Constancia's neighborhood. Spring is in the air. Your windows go up with a bang that is everything but studied and proper; you shout across the airshaft to your neighbor; you don't know her very well, but you ask her why she doesn't come over sometime; she promises to do so; you bring a pillow and place it on the window ledge; you lean there happy, drinking in the sun, telling your neighbor all your business, learning all hers. It is good to gossip; it is fine to feel the spring.

If it keeps up like this you are going to take off that heavy underwear tomorrow. If tonight is as warm as last night you will take your pillows down and sit on the stoop. What a summer it will be if spring is like this! You don't think you will go to Mrs. Cohen's today. There is something independent in your blood. You have your own work, your own spring cleaning to do. Let Mrs. Cohen get somebody else for a day, or do without. At least she will do without *you*. Spring has declared a holiday. Not only for you, but for many others. The street below is suddenly warm and dark with life, where yesterday it was cold and deserted. It takes but a breath of spring to bring these dark bees out of their hives to sip at the warm, pestiferous flowers of the city. The drones are happy. In loud boisterous groups they collect on the street corners; they swap yarns, and invent lies, embroidering them with solemn faces masked with every semblance of verisimilitude. You would think them the happiest people under the sun, and for the moment they are, as their laughter, unrestrained and strident, mounts up through the slits in the fireescape. Out in the back yards some are singing, the only sort of work they will ever do, able-bodied men and women hiding underneath dark glasses eyes which can probe the night, masking the strength of their legs in a painful halt which a veteran actor would envy, raising their deceitful voices in rich harmony for the few pennies which you throw them grudgingly, because at heart you know there is no truth in their blindness, only miming in their lameness.

Spring takes some slowly, easing into them and accepting from them the slow consciousness of warmth with which a snake, frozen all winter long, begins slowly to change from harmless rigidity to a final deadly quickness. But others are taken suddenly, like Sam; besieged by restlessness, the world becomes a prison for them, and they begin to look around for any hidden means of escape. Anything that savors of duty and routine becomes torture. A traveling man more than any other resents the daily come and go, the similarity of each succeeding day, the paucity of unchanging nights. And there is no worse goad than memory, to show him how bare today's existence is in comparison with yesterday's.

What most you loved you begin most to hate, to find fault with, to search a reason for abandoning. And there is no torture worse than endeavoring to hate when at heart you know there is cause only for love; nothing as contemptible as trying to pick a quarrel when there is reason for nothing but peace; nothing more cowardly than leaving

when every reason you advance bids you stick to
your guns.

And if in spite of all you remain, like Sam, it
is at the cost of too much in the end. Living becomes an endless array of petty quarrels, tears, recriminations, pleas for forgiveness, torrential moments of fierce physical attempts at atonement,
which leave one happy and exhausted, but no happier on the morrow.

With a growing uneasiness in which he could
scent a presentiment of evil Sam watched the di-
vergent ways of his path and of Mattie's widen;
the farther he looked into the distance the more
apart they were. And try as he could, there was no
way of denying that the way of both was of his own
choosing. Mattie's whole life lay wrapped in a
white handkerchief and laid carefully away in a
drawer. She had made a shrine of his cards and his
razor. The magic would never depart from them
for her. She had erected a temple to them; they
were as much to her as leaves from the burning
bush might have been. It sent a chill through Sam
as he watched her from time to time with the cards
spread out before her, the razor laid alongside
them, and her dark lovely head bent above them,
in silent inexplicable communion, her lips moving in prayer and petition. Whenever they quar-
reled she went to her talismans; and though Sam

hated them, and scorned them, and knew better than anyone alive that there was no virtue in them, he had neither the heart nor the courage to destroy them.

He knew how much they meant to Mattie. He never would forget the first time he had realized how much they meant. It was during the cold period when he just could not get his will together enough to face the wind in search of work; when despite the silent protest on Mattie's face, despite the half-serious recriminations of Aunt Mandy, he had spent his days beside the fire, playing cards with Aunt Mandy. One day two of the cards had been swept from the table in a sudden gust of high merriment by Aunt Mandy, as she laughed at some outlandish witticism with which Sam was currying her favor; the cards had fallen into the fire and been burned. The deck was useless without the missing members; and Sam suddenly thought of Mattie's cards hidden away in their room in the dresser drawer.

"Suppose we use Mattie's cards?" he queried.

Aunt Mandy had hesitated for a moment, for she knew the store Mattie set by those cards. But in her sight Mattie's cards were more of an abomination than her own. She did not like the way Mattie pored over them, "making a brazen image out of them, like the golden calf," as Aunt Mandy expressed it. It was wrong; it was sinful. And so she had said nothing to deter Sam from getting them.

The game went on amid that laughter and raillery which bound Sam and Aunt Mandy together. They were so engrossed in their battle that they did not hear Mattie enter; and it was only when they looked up, to find her staring at them in anger and sorrow, that they looked down guiltily at the cards in their hands. Sam would never forget Mattie's look as she silently gathered up the pack, nor her voice as she turned on the threshold to tell them, "I'd be ashamed to do a thing like that, and afraid God would strike me dead."

And that night she held him close as if she were afraid some evil spirit would enter the room and bear him off; while in his heart had died forever the thought of revealing to her how little blessed those cards were, how deeply cursed that razor. She would be able to understand that a converted man could backslide, but never that one could play with God as he had done. He remembered the minister's words, "She'd hate the church and me and you."

There is no telling to what depths of despair and everlasting unbelief Mattie might have been hurled had she discovered how small a part the hand of heaven had played in her conversion, how devoid of heat, how lacking in chill, how absolutely neutral had been the fingers of fire and ice which she had felt playing along her spine the morning she came through. Those who are born to their religion, accepting it passively because their fathers before them bowed to the same god, or those who enter in the full possession of their faculties, after having weighed the good and evil points, are not subject to that exaggerated devotion which comes with a miracle. Though Mattie's life had been simple in the extreme, having in it nothing that might be called sinful, more serious than the absence of her name on the church register, with her conversion came all the horror of little sins and all the sudden holiness which made Sam's life a martyrdom.

She saw in her conversion the white and glistening hand of God; and after the night of her wedding, when for a moment to please Sam she had bowed to love and had danced, she danced no more, save for Christ. Young as she was she entered into the life of Mount Hebron with a piety and an assiduity which put many of the veteran sisters and brothers to shame. She never missed a class-meeting or a prayer-service, and Sunday was one long interminable attendance at church. People began to look forward to hearing her speak at testimonial time; for all the fervent sayings which she had heard year after year while attending church as a sinner now came to mind, and were spoken with downcast eyes, in a voice conscious of the unworthiness of the speaker, yet with a firmness which marked young Sister Lucas as one who would go far in the church.

Sam backslid gently but firmly, and after a month of church attendance ceased to be a practicing Christian, and though Mattie laid him on the altar morning after morning, it was of no avail.

The sort of job Constancia had secured for Sam had made matters worse, and Mattie soon came to feel that it would be better to perish than to gain their living as her husband did his as a doorkeeper in the tents of the wicked. For once, passing by the theater, she had seen one of the women performers resting in the little court which led to the stage door. The woman, fawn-brown in complexion, was gaudy in a harrowing, feline way, with high arched eyebrows, vividly-painted lips, and a sleekness about her that made Mattie tremble for Sam, who stood in the theater door, gayly garnering tickets. Sometimes Sam brought her things which he found in the dressing-rooms of those women after they had gone on to another theater—bits of ribbon, a comb, a rhinestone buckle. She never dared ask him how he came by these things, and though she took them, she never used them.

One night he returned home, happily rousing her out of sleep with a frightening bellow into her ear, holding up for her approval a bright-red kimona which one of the women had left. She could see in his eyes that he admired it, thought it fine, and felt that it was a real gift. But the nature of it, the intimacy of it, a too familiar gesture in Sam's fingers as they fondled it, frightened and hurt her. She took the kimona in her hand, but an odor of stale perfume made her drop the garment as if a scorpion had stung her. "I can't wear that," she said, turning away from him and hiding her face against the wall. "It would make me feel cheap and common."

Sam had not been able to understand, and the rejection of his gift had filled him with slow anger. He had let it lie on the floor, where it lay shining like something malevolent, as he silently undressed and climbed into bed. He had not taken her in his arm nor kissed her, but they had slept back to back in sullen distrust of one another.

Mattie had forgotten the incident the next morning. It happened to be Sam's day off, and Constancia was letting her free a half-day also, in order that she might do something which she had long desired to do. She had wanted to invite Reverend Drummond to have dinner with her and Sam. Sam had consented, even if none too graciously. The crimson kimona caught Mattie's eyes as she leaped out of bed lightly so as not to awaken Sam; she took the offending garment up gingerly and thrust it away in the clothes closet. She bent over and kissed Sam before setting out for her half-day at Constancia's.

She had counted on Sam to help her with the dinner, at least to be near her and to talk to her. But when she came home aglow with the prospect of entertaining her spiritual adviser, Aunt Mandy informed her that Sam had gone out soon after breakfast and had not indicated when he would return. She had thought nothing of it, and had continued gayly with the preparations for her dinner. She had bought the best her money could buy. Reverend Drummond seldom dined with his members, and it was only after much pleading that he had consented to dine with her. Mattie felt decidedly happy.

The afternoon passed; all the preparations had been made; the dinner sang and hissed on the stove; the table was a thing of beauty. Aunt Mandy and Mattie were happy. They only wished Sam would hurry home. He would hardly have time to wash and spruce up a bit before the minister would be there. It was already within half an hour of the time. And then Sam had come in. Mattie turned to meet him, took a few joyous steps toward him, before she stopped transfixed with all her heaven toppling about her. He had embalmed his anger in liquor, and now stood before her evil and unforgiving. She tried to lead him to the bedroom and coax him to sleep; but he was not drunk to the point of being inoffensive. He had merely taken enough to be disagreeable and vengeful. Pushing her aside, he had staggered to the closet, where he had retrieved the unappreciated kimona.

Pleading had been of no avail, nor tears. When Reverend Drummond, kindly and hungry, entered, he found two sorrowing, shame-stricken women making apologies for the head of the house, who sat with his dirty shoes resting on the edge of the white tablecloth, and over his knees a scarlet kimona.

The minister had not wavered; if anything, his eyes had flickered with amusement, as he blessed the table, with Sam's feet still high in the air. He was a man of tact, and his grace was not only that of the church. He had talked kindly to Sam, had assured him that the kimona was pretty, and had even exacted from Mattie a promise to wear it. "That is not too much of a sacrifice in order to keep peace in one's home," he had said. And he had made them kiss, and had thrown back his head and laughed uproariously at them as they did so.

Then gently the minister had leaned over and eased Sam's feet from the table.

As Sam ate, his clouded brain began to freshen up and he soon felt that the minister wasn't so bad a person, after all. He was jolly despite the cut of his cloth, and left them little time to mope as he regaled them with story after story. One in particular had made them laugh until the tears ran down their faces.

"These young preachers have it easy," Reverend Drummond explained. "They should have come along in my time when a man had to be worth his salt and had to have more than the grace of God in him to win and keep a congregation. Now most of them come to churches that are ready to receive them with courtesy at least, if not with open arms. I wonder what they would do if they had to meet a congregation like my first one. They required preaching of the rousing kind, and in order to get it they never kept a preacher longer than two years. Every new preacher was subjected to a real test. When he went to the church to preach his first sermon, no one welcomed him. The entire congregation greeted him seated with their backs turned away from him. They could not see him. The test required that in order to keep the charge he had to preach so vigorously that by the time he ended more than half the congregation had turned around to look him in the face. That called for *preaching!*"

"And how did you come through," Sam asked, with glistening eyes; for there was something in this story that made him think there were more ways to heaven than one, and that his cards and razor might not be as bad as they were painted.

Reverend Drummond leaned back and laughed. "I won them all," he said, "but I ended up with my coat and collar at my feet. And they kept me five years."

After the minister had gone, Mattie took off her company clothes and decked herself in the scarlet kimona. Sam stumbled around unsteadily, helping her to clear the table. They had never been happier.

Chapter Twelve

W HAT will women not do for this man called Jesus? What have they not done for Him? What will they not expend in time and money and love to spread His story, to win Him converts, to build Him houses, to rout all other gods before Him? The women have always been more faithful to Him than the men. Think only on Mary Magdalene and that ointment which might have been sold to feed the poor, as practical, male-thinking Judas wanted to do; think of the three women who went to the tomb for His body while the men were still deep in inactive sorrow. What and whom will a woman not sacrifice, forsake, insult, make a target for shame, for His kingdom's sake? Think on Mattie.

Shame and misery encircled her like a shroud, pressed in upon her and disturbed her waking hours, kept her suffocated and dream-ridden at night. The man through whom she had come to her Saviour was steadily slipping away, slowly and without any effort to save himself, sinking back into the ways of sinners. Mattie felt weak and companionless as she went to church Sunday after Sunday, and to meeting after meeting, alone or with Aunt Mandy, but never at her side that man whose sudden but brief conversion had set the church on fire, had sent tremors of fire and ice coursing along her spine. She could hardly speak for shame when they inquired about him. She felt that she would die beneath the slow Christian smiles that were half sympathy and half derision as they shook their heads and clucked their tongues. With deep loyalty she explained that a man must work, that he cannot always choose his occupation, and that Sam was obliged to toil on Sundays. And then on his one night free he was tired. The thought struck her, "Too tired to serve his Jesus!" And she determined that at all costs she must put her arms under him, whether he willed it or not, and extricate him from the quagmire into which he was sinking.

If only she could get him to church again, she thought, some power in the atmosphere, some breath of divine air, might fan his cheek, might blow into his heart and stir to fire again the dead ashes there. She dared not ask him directly and openly, nor reproach him too earnestly with his apostasy. For something intuitive and part of her womanly equipment told her that his mind and feet were wavering on a line, and that it needed

little for him to cross it and to be off and gone
forever. Yet she felt that the only way of fastening
him securely to his life with her lay in getting him
back into the fold.

Delilah pleading to know where Samson's
strength lay hidden; Salome dancing for John's
head; Mattie determined that Sam should not lose
his soul: Three women, one with a glib tongue,
one with twinkling feet, and one burning with
religion; all three armed with the asp of coquetry.

Sam on his day off lay sprawled upon the bed,
watching Mattie as she slipped into her clothes.
Sun filtered through the windows and made him
throw back the covers. He pitied Mattie that she
could not lie abed with him. Peace and contentment and the promise of rest lay on his black handsome face. Something in the day and the season
stirred him to a consciousness that Mattie was as
lovely as ever. He tugged at her dress. Looking
around at him, she felt and knew the love that was
keeping him there with her in spite of himself.
But first and foremost came her Lord Jesus.

She bent and kissed Sam fervently. Caught and
locked in the grip of his arm, she stroked his head,
whispering, "Love me?"

He lay with his head on her bosom, lay laughing
and smiling up at her, as he answered only with his
eyes, but in unspoken words that held no negative.

"Then promise me something," she went on, hurrying lest he interrupt her. "Let us go out together tonight. It's been a long time since you've been out with me. Promise."

To Sam going out meant joy, people, laughter, music; something to which Mattie had not given herself since their wedding night. He smiled happily, and squeezed her as he said: "I promise. Where?"

"Somewhere I want to go," said Mattie, evasively.

"All right." Sam turned over, happy and sleepy again.

That evening Mattie maintained her air of secrecy, dressed herself with a touch of spirit, while Sam chose his tie sprinkled with yellow stars. As they sauntered out into the warm Harlem air, Mattie prayed to Heaven to meet her halfway. Sam was lost in dreams and in the feel of Mattie close to him, the bright lights and the high hearty laughter of his people all about him. He walked as if he were a poet thinking on immortal lines instead of a ticket-chopper out for an evening stroll. It was only when they stood under the great white light of the church that he realized where she had been leading him. He drew back scowling, one reluctant foot already poised on the church step. Mattie braced herself for the combat.

"Not on my evening out. I don't call that a holi-day, nor an evening out, going to church," Sam protested. Mattie could feel his arm stiffen beneath her light pressure.

"You promised," she pleaded, meeting his disgusted stare with a look all injury and ill treatment.

Angrily he pushed her ahead of him, and entered the church. Mattie felt that the first skirmish had been won, as they took their seats, while people, remembering Sam, pointed him out and whispered his story. Despite the warm weather, the church was well filled for the prayer service. Aunt Mandy, to whom Mattie had not confided her hope of getting Sam to the meeting, was already there, rocking back and forth and moaning beautifully.

The meeting promised to be one of the best. The music was good; the hymns chosen were the rollicking kind; the spirits of the audience seemed to mount higher as if each hymn and testimonial were the rung of a ladder which was taking them nearer and nearer to that Beulah land of which they sang. The testimonials were frank and flagellant; each speaker seemed to find a special joy in open confession, in announcing to all the world his unworthiness as a partaker of life and the many joys which Jesus was showering upon him. In each voice was a fierce knout with which they scourged themselves. There was not one there who seemed to feel that he had a right to joy and laughter. They all, according to their own admission, were steeped in sin. Their only hope was that Christ's blood might cleanse them.

Sam alone sat sullen and unmoved, brooding through half-closed eyes, eaten up with anger that Mattie should have tricked him into coming there. Beside him Mattie sat communing with Heaven as she had done the day of their first Communion together. Then they had been, as she had thought, entering upon a new and beautiful life together. Now her lips were moving in a silent petition that Christ stoop down and gather up once more into the palm of His hand this man whom she loved.

Time was passing, and Sam had not joined in on one hymn, nor spoken one word for his Jesus. To Mattie's timid suggestion that he testify he had merely mumbled something under his breath about leading a horse to water but not being able to make him drink.

At last, silently calling Heaven to her aid, Mattie rose to testify for them both.

All eyes were turned upon her as she stood there ready to speak, for that glory which they had wanted to expend on Sam had, after his defection, been transferred to Mattie; she was now an acquisition toward whom the church pointed with pride, even if with pity, on account of her backsliding husband.

"Brothers and sisters"—she spoke so low at first as to be almost inaudible—"the Lord has done great things for me, and His praise is forever in my mouth. He has withheld no good thing from me. I have given Him my word, and I can't turn back."

"Amen, child," breathed Aunt Mandy, fervently, from her seat in the amen corner, among the aging handmaidens of the Lord.

"There is only one thing I am asking of the Lord," Mattie went on, her words coming with a rush as if she must get them out quickly or they would not come at all. She turned and bent her eyes full on Sam, and there was such devotion in them as would not be downed by the seething anger with which he looked up at her. "I want Christ to reach down and take my husband back into His fold."

The church held its breath. Here on a plain meeting night was drama that by rights belonged only to revival time.

Sam felt as if all the curious, pitying eyes turned on him were so many stones; he shrank down into his seat as if to ward them off. Still through his misery he could hear his wife's ecstatic, fervent voice: "Reach down, O Lord, and turn him back into the path which leads to glory. Before death's sickle cuts him down, take him back, Heavenly Father, into your fold!" The church loomed up before him as one vast accusing eye, as one great voice pleading for his redemption. He could bear no more. Suddenly he arose, not to seek the altar as once he had done, but to push brutally past Mattie and to make his way toward the door. An usher who made as if to bar his way suddenly stepped aside as he saw the hot shame and the unreasoning bitterness on Sam's face.

Mattie stood defeated as a certain minister had done; and no miracle came to her aid.

Chapter Thirteen

TO MATTIE'S surprise, Aunt Mandy, that stanch Christian, had sided wholly with Sam. She always contended that it was Mattie's open prayer which goaded Sam on to Emma May. It wasn't decent, she argued, to air one's family wash in church as Mattie had done. In one's secret closet, yes, with only one's God to hear, one might ask for anything, strip one's life and soul bare, but in open church, that was a different matter. She, for one, felt that Sam had behaved as any outraged and humiliated man would have acted under like circumstances, when he had informed Mattie afterwards at home, "You'll never shame me again; I never hopes to enter church again unless they brings me in feet first." In vain Mattie had thrust a too tardy hand up to his mouth in an endeavour to stem his blasphemy; the words were out. And although she had cried half through the night, Sam, lost and unrepentant, had slept soundly at her side.

There was a bond between Aunt Mandy and Sam which the old lady herself could not explain, but which seemed to tighten with no perceptible effort, and to relegate Mattie to a second place in her aunt's affections. Sam sometimes felt tempted to tell the old lady the real story of his conversion, he was sure that she would have laughed in spite of her disapproval.

With ever-deepening distress, Mattie beheld the forces of evil working against her. Aunt Mandy, who, until Sam had entered on his job as doorman at the Star Movie Palace, had never beheld any cinema performance save stereopticon views of the "Suffering and Death of Christ," became a devotee of this sinful new amusement. Sam was not doorman for nothing, and Aunt Mandy was filled with pride and importance because she was able to come to the theater at will, and to enter gratuitously simply because her tall, elegantly-attired nephew was there to wave her in with a grandeur which might easily have been mistaken for ownership.

Now that her afternoon game of cards had been lost to her by Sam's work, Aunt Mandy hastened feverishly each morning to tidy up the house in order that she might be at the theater almost as early as Sam. It mattered not to her that she must often see the same performance over and over again; in each showing there was always something to laugh at anew, or something which she had

missed in the previous representation. Sam con-
trived to keep a seat in the back row ever available
for his crony, and there she would perch, like a
little wizened yellow bird, looking with happy
eyes on worlds of which she had never dreamed
before. From time to time, as business slackened,
Sam would leave his post at the door and come
over to talk to her, to her infinite delight and belief in her growing importance.

It began to be rumored at Mount Hebron that
Aunt Mandy was falling off in her Christian duties; for now, as often as not, although she might
leave home in the evening with her mind sternly
set on the prayer-meeting at Mount Hebron, she
was likely to end up at the Star Palace. Mattie felt
as if her Aunt and Sam had entered into a con-
spiracy against her.

Sam was not as loving as he had formerly been.
The spontaneity and the fire of his affection
seemed to have cooled, and no graciousness or
studied attempt on Mattie's part was able to revive
it. Mattie remembered the disturbing beauty of
the show woman whom she had seen in the theater
alley one day, and she shuddered.

But she had cast her net of suspicions too high;
she needed to aim lower and nearer than at the
fleeting, flashily dressed show girls who were only
transient beams in Sam's eyesight. She knew noth-

ing of Emma May's conquest until Aunt Mandy told her.

For some time Aunt Mandy had been watching Sam and Emma May, and pitying Mattie.

Though Aunt Mandy realized that a natural intimacy must exist between the lone usher of a small theater and the doorman, there were certain glances and signs, too frequent whisperings, sudden bursts of laughter with something shameful in them, which she felt did not proceed from business relations. For one thing, Aunt Mandy thought Emma May might have found other means of passing her time when there was no one to usher to a seat, than by chatting with Sam and keeping him away from her; and there was the too frank and too open way in which Emma May would stand with her light-brown hand on Sam's shoulder. A light, indifferent touch, perhaps, but to Aunt Mandy that small brown hand was a talon of possession. There was, moreover, a crude voluptuousness about Emma May which aroused Aunt Mandy's enmity and distrust; she felt as if Emma May could have and ought to have done something to check the sinister flowering of her attractions. The old lady disliked the pagan roundness of the usherette; the massive gold hoops in Emma May's ears were vulgar, not small and decent like her own. That gold tooth in Emma May's

mouth was a deliberate decoy, as were the bracelets jangling with her every movement, and the
scent of diluted perfume which always heralded
her appearance. Emma May always passed the
time of day with her, but Aunt Mandy, too dis-
trustful to be polite, would never respond.

And as Mattie wilted, Emma May blossomed
and insolently tightened the grasp of her round,
brown hand on Sam's shoulder. Aunt Mandy
looked on with sorrow, but in silence; for there
was nothing concrete on which she could base her
suspicions. These unproven suspicions made her
querulous and argumentative with Mattie. She
tried to arouse her niece out of the lethargy into
which her religion was drowning her. "Praying
won't stop a man what's slipping away to other
women. You have to win him back with something
quicker than that," said the old lady, her eyes half
hinting a wisdom which she was afraid to broach
to her God-fearing niece.

"What's quicker or more powerful than prayer,
Aunt Mandy?" Mattie asked, so piteously that her
aunt risked the suggestion that had been so long
quivering on her tongue.

"Sometimes when the angels is too busy to help
you, you have to fight the devil with his own
tools," the old lady broadened the hint, but only
slightly. She had begun to stand in awe of the

righteous, church-going Mattie whose simon-pure religion made the old lady feel that she herself was the sorriest backslider in the world. Aunt Mandy was not going to come out plainly with what was behind the mystic simplicity of her words until Mattie should invite explanation by a show of sympathetic interest.

"There isn't anything more powerful than prayer, and what Heaven won't do, hell can't," said Mattie, despairingly. "Yet," she continued, plaintively, "if I knew some certain way to get Sam back, and loving the way he used to be, I think I'd try it."

There was such misery and hopelessness in the thin black visage which looked up from Mattie's cupped hands that Aunt Mandy let the die fall. "I know a woman," she said, eagerly, "who can tell what's going to happen, and change it. She can mix a powder strong enough to win any man back."

But Mattie had not reached the brink of despair, as her aunt could see, even though there lay between her and that bottomless pit but a few scant steps which she was steadily diminishing with a sure, if with an unconscious, step. She looked up at her aunt with all the fine scorn of which she was capable. "You mean conjuring, don't you, Aunt Mandy?" she inquired. "I haven't come to that yet. I still have Jesus."

Proud and sorrowing, bolstered up only by her faith and by the sudden realization of life growing within her, too proud to speak to Sam of that life which was as much his as hers, she watched him ease down from an ardent lover to the level of a perfunctory husband. He became now merely the man who shared her household, but all the magic and soaring of loving was gone.

And Mattie could not lay her finger on the sore.

There were nights when Sam did not come home at all, nights when Mattie tossed about in sleepless worry until Sam returned just early enough to snatch a few hours' sleep before being off to work. Mattie was too proud to ask an explanation and Sam vouchsafed none.

Aunt Mandy berated Sam whenever she had him alone for a moment; but he treated her with a good-humored condescension that let her angry words fall from him as water from a duck's back. When she upbraided him and threw Emma May's name at him, he only laughed softly and whistled through his teeth at her.

Finally, Aunt Mandy could stand Mattie's pain-racked, pining face no longer. After all, Mattie was her niece and blood *was* thicker than water.

And she told Mattie about Emma May, while

Mattie listened in a pathetic silence which went straight to Aunt Mandy's heart.

"I remember her," said Mattie, simply. "She is very pretty."

And that had been all. She had said no more. Aunt Mandy had been so annoyed that she had wanted to slap Mattie. It was all right to be religious and lost in the inner life, she felt, but there were things in this other life which were important. And loving was one. She never could have confirmed another woman's beauty as Mattie had done, if it had been a question of Ben. Though she lost all Paradise for it, she would have done something about it.

Mattie was not the confiding kind, however; and underneath her righteousness the primitive slept a not eternal sleep. All day the lively brown face of Emma May stayed before her, leaped in and out of her path like a dancing demon; the loud, uncouth laughter of Emma May ran out of the kitchen faucet and hissed out of the steam of the kettle. Emma May's gold hoops disturbed her during the night; they became large bands of steel which bound and squeezed her until she awoke, ashy with terror, drenched with fright, to find day streaming in upon her and no Sam at her side.

Man has yet to raise up a stronger god than

Eros. The wood of the cross is poisoned by his venomous arrow.

Mattie decided that she would go to Emma May. If Sam were there, too, so much the better. She would confront them together. Even in the midst of her heart-break, custom was strong upon her, and she knelt to pray before leaving the house. She knew that Emma May, besides being usher at the Star Palace, was also obliged to do the early-morning dusting. She wrapped herself in a light spring coat, although it was hot enough to go without an outer wrap. That coat was to serve a purpose; for under it she concealed, clutched close to her bosom, a small sharp hatchet. Taking it was an intuitive, unstudied gesture, an obedience to the hypnotic suggestion of a cold, unreasoning fury.

The doors of the Star Palace were open wide. As Mattie entered, she could hear Emma May's low humming as she went from row to row, dusting the hard wooden chairs. Even in her workday clothes, a plain gingham apron and a dust-cap on her head, Emma May was pretty. The gold hoops made shining arcs on either side of her face, and from underneath the dust-cap a twist of thick black hair had crept, to form a curl on her forehead. Mattie stood in the doorway and watched her for a moment. There was no sign of Sam.

Emma May looked up to find Mattie confronting her.

Emma May had never seen Mattie before, but she knew it was Mattie and she waited.

The jungles produce no thing that hates another with a hate more deadly than that with which Mattie hated Emma May.

"You are Emma May," said Mattie.

Emma May rested a light-brown hand on one of the chairs with that same inoppressiveness which was still like the clutch of possession with which Aunt Mandy had seen her lay her hands on Sam.

Emma May did not answer.

"I am Sam's wife," said Mattie.

Still Emma May did not reply; only her brown eyes meeting Mattie's squarely responded with unspoken and bitter mockery. Suddenly the mockery died in the bright eyes as a slim black hand swept up and closed over the fawn-brown throat; with her other hand Mattie hugged the hatchet close to her bosom.

Gone was the gentle servitor of the gentlest of all the gods. The primitive woman, she whose skin is neither white nor black, she who is older than her Jesus, looked out of Mattie's blazing eyes and spoke with her rasping tongue. "Was he with you last night?"

Emma May was helpless in the furious grip, and, more than that, desperately lost in that fright which fleshy women have in the presence and strength of their leaner, fiercer sisters. She could only nod her head and gurgle an acquiescence, until Mattie released her and sent her stumbling against one of the seats.

They stood eying one another for a moment, while Mattie's anger subsided as quickly as it had risen, until only shame and confusion covered her at the thought of what she, a church-going, God-fearing Christian had done, and of the wilder, more fearful thing she had contemplated, but had not carried through. She opened her coat from the seclusion of which the hatchet fell with a dull thud to lie between her feet and Emma May's. She wanted to ask Emma May's forgiveness. She wanted to get away to herself and weep. She wanted to pray to her Jesus. She wanted Aunt Mandy's arm around her. She wanted Sam. She wanted anything except the thought of what she had meant to do, of how she had intended to scar Emma May's too pretty fawn-brown face. She slowly gathered her coat about her and walked away. As she reached the door she turned, and caught sight of Emma May turning the hatchet about in her hands in fright and perplexity.

Mattie felt as if she were like a wounded cat

dragging itself to a caressing hand as she made her way to Constancia's. Constancia did not fail her. She quickly noted the dull, bewildered gaze, the slackness of the usual deft hands, the low-pitched, unintonated responses to her sallies. Constancia, into whose life adoration had dropped like a rich red plum shaken from some celestial tree, still had that ineradicable feminine thought that a man is at the root of every woman's slightest suffering.

"Is it Sam, Mattie?" Constancia asked, all the raillery fled from her cloudless amber eyes, and nothing left there but solicitude for her maid's happiness.

"Somewhat," was Mattie's loyal and non-committal response.

"Too black and handsome," said Constancia as she shook her head in pity. "An evil combination."

When she returned home that evening, Mattie knew that Sam had not been there at all during the day. She had no heart for anything. She held her breath for fear he had gone forever, although she derived some consolation from the thought that his clothes were still there, and that he would have to come to fetch them, should he be leaving. By now he knew of her visit to Emma May. She wondered how he would take it. She didn't care, if only he wouldn't leave.

Seated at the front window, she looked down at

the sweating, swarming mass of life strutting and posturing, laughing in the face of the sweltering June heat, and she too laughed inwardly as she thought of the growing, rounding bit of life which she would add to that below, a life of which she had not yet told Sam, lest he think it but a trick to win him back to his sweet ways with her. She closed her eyes in happy contemplation of that blossoming, unborn bit of black humanity.

Hearing the door bang, she started up from her dreaming, fearful and anxious; but it was only Aunt Mandy, who had gone to meeting for a change and who had returned. The old lady was tired. She knew nothing of the day's happenings, but she had plumbed the depths of Mattie's unhappiness at Sam's absence from home. She went over and kissed her niece and patted her sleek black cheek.

"Don't worry, honey," she admonished her. "It will all come out right in the end." And she had dragged her weary limbs into bed.

Mattie sat by the window awhile longer, dreaming of her first meeting with Sam, thinking back to the evangelist and his gentleness, of her refusal to heed his petitions until Sam had shown her the way; surely that evening had not revealed itself as a precursor to the misery of the present moment. She rose and went into their bedroom, where, too tired and anxious to sleep, she sat by the window and gazed out into the dismal airshaft on which the bedroom gave, as if some glimmering fairy landscape lay revealed there. Drowsiness came down and conquered her, and she sat there lost in sleep until she was awakened by the feeling of some one there in the room with her. As her eyes fought back their still sleep-laden lids, she knew it was Sam. He was stumbling about in the room, and his breath invaded the narrow confines of their chamber with a stench of whisky that sickened her. She watched him for a moment, too utterly happy that he had come home to think of upbraiding him. She sat silent and jubilant, immersed in the simple contentment of his presence.

She did not even move when she saw him lurch to the dresser and fling open the drawer in which she kept her talismans.

Only when her sacred cards were flung to the floor, and when she saw in Sam's hand the razor which he had not touched since the night of her conversion, did she catch her breath and clutch her throat to keep from screaming. With horrified eyes she saw him heave toward the bed, saw the open razor flash in his hand, up and down, up and down, like an arc of moonlight; she heard the thin summer sheets crack as the sharp blade slit them through. She heard the rip of the mattress until

she could bear no more. It was as if he had slit
her heart, as he had meant to do. She knew now
what a cruel vengeance he had wanted to exact for
her visit to Emma May. In abject pity of herself,
she watched him as he swayed above the bed, panting and drunkenly satisfied.

"Sam!" She could scarcely recognize her own
voice, it was so low, so lifeless and bare. He reeled
around in amazement not comprehending that she
was still there and that he had only demolished
the bedding instead of her warm, too clinging
flesh.

It did not matter now what happened to her.
Those strokes had been meant for her. She went
over to him. Now that his fury was spent, he was
like a small boy who has been caught in mischief.
No thought of what he had meant to do lingered
with him.

"You meant that for me, Sam, didn't you?" She
did not know why she was asking him to confirm
what she too plainly knew. Tears welled in her
eyes, but did not fall.

Suddenly anger that her love meant so little
to him overcame her, as she thought of the child
she was carrying. With a quick, hot hand she
reached up and ripped open her shirt and under-
garment, until her bare black bosom gleamed out
at him with its faint, yet already visible, signs of

her coming motherhood. She took his hand and placed it on the mound. "You would have killed me and your baby," she told him. "And afterwards you would have swung!"

The next moment he was at her feet, sobbing, and she was bending over him, stroking the hard tight balls on his head. At their feet the cards were scattered across the room like the ribs of a huge fan, bound together by strips of carpet. And close by, forgotten and useless, as harmless now as it had been hateful a moment past, gleamed the razor.

He held her close as if he would keep her against all the world, and she felt a salvation greater than Heaven's pin him to her.

Later she gathered up the scattered strips of their sheets and thrust them with a tremor into the closet. The mattress had been ripped apart so badly that it would have to be sewn together before they slept on it. Sam watched her get the needle and coarse black thread; like a sorry, beaten dog he followed her with his eyes as she made ready to sew up the rents. Lumberingly he stumbled over to the bed, where he knelt down and aided her to stuff the straw back into the cheap mattress; and then he helped her hold the mattress-covering taut so she could sew it. This was his peace offering. She accepted it as she would have taken a rainbow as a sign that only fair days were to follow.

He held her to him that night as he had not done for many nights past. The last thing she remembered before falling to sleep was the thick sound of his voice, saying, "A little baby, a little black baby, like me and you."

Chapter Fourteen

SUMMER had gone, and with it all that summer held.

Mattie lay on the parlor divan, thinking what
hopes that high season had held for the chill days
that were now upon her, and how cruelly the cold
had ransacked her small house of warmth, chilling
its lone occupant. All summer long she had held
Sam by a thread, a thread so thin that she had
trembled to think of its insecurity; but she had
laughed to feel it hold more insistently every day.
When that thread should break at last it would
mean the beginning of a life to which Sam would
be forever anchored and stayed, from which Emma
May would never be able to entice him. She had
known all along that she had not wholly defeated
Emma May. There had been intervals when she
had felt Emma May tugging away at her fragile
happiness, but hope had always revived in her as
she had watched Sam's face light up whenever he
talked of the son he was sure she was carrying for
him. . . . Lying on the divan now, watching the
fire curl up in the stove opposite her, she fingered

absently the cheap black dress she was wearing, as she thought with bitterness of the dreams she had watched grow in Sam's heart at the thought of his son. It had amused him highly to think how black the child would be, coming from them, the utter distillation of race. It had been fun to see Sam build and demolish his great air castles, to hear him choose and reject the work his son was to do; no rounder like himself—not his boy; he would be a doctor or a lawyer or a teacher, something fine. "And when he's rich and great," Sam had said over and over again with his son's destiny in his eyes, "as black as he'll be, nobody will be able to say it's on account of his white blood, because there ain't a drop between you and me." And Mattie had sat at his side, matching dream with dream, feeling the thread by which she held him grow stronger, seeing in the distance the gold hoops and bright eyes of Emma May pass into nothingness. . . .

All that was passed now. Of it all nothing remained more tanglible than this black dress which she was wearing for a dead baby toward whom she had been too weak and pain-racked to turn her eyes. All that was gone, but she would never forget Sam's snarling, disappointed face as she had smiled up at him in her pain, not knowing then that the thread had been too brittle; nor his voice that had crushed her into a deadly coma when he had cried out, "Not able even to born a baby!" And he had gone. Back to Emma May. That had been years ago, hadn't it? No, only a few weeks. He had not come back once. He had not seen the baby buried. Aunt Mandy alone had attended to that. Sam had offered the old lady money when she passed by the theater, to plead with him to return; but he had said that he was through with a house where there was so much religion and so little strength. . . . Mattie had sent the money back proudly. Mrs. Brandon would not let her want. Her strength would soon return. She had never seen the right-eous suffering nor their seed begging bread. Her friends at Mount Hebron had been good with gifts of money and food. And Aunt Mandy was still not too old to do a little day's work. Let him keep his money and spend it on Emma May. . . .

Pride wields a bitter tongue, but love eats bitter bread. . . .

Fingering her black dress, she heard the low, suffering voice of affection drowning the strident voice of pride. She knew there was nothing in the world that she regretted losing so much as Sam. The dead baby was a stranger whom she had never known, no more to her now than a wound that had closed and healed over, of which memory was the only scar; but Sam was the man Heaven had sent her, to whom Heaven had intrusted her salvation, through whom she had gone to Jesus. Tied in a white handkerchief laid away in the dresser drawer of their deserted room were her talismans, still holding their glory.

She must stop this daydreaming. Aunt Mandy would soon be home from her day's work; it would soon be time to eat, and then to sleep another lonely night away. With less effort than she had thought it would take, she lifted herself from the divan. She seemed to feel the glow and warmth of life which had been suspended in her these past three weeks, quicken and begin to flow as if a slow, reviving liquid were being poured into her dusty veins. She would soon be able to go to Mount Hebron again, where she had not been since a few weeks before her confinement. Perhaps prayer in the house of the Lord would prove stronger than in one's own little apartment. She would pray for Sam's return; she would pray for Emma May, not for her hurt in any way, but that she might turn from her sinful living. She paused a moment, to lean against the side of the table, a plate poised in her wasted black hand, while a recurring thought of which she had not been able to rid herself these last days danced impishly before her. Were there really some things which Heaven could not do, that unholy men and women could bring about with a drop of liquid, or a pill dropped into one's coffee? Her dark cheeks burned at the memory of a conversation she had had with Aunt Mandy soon after Sam's departure. The old lady had been sitting beside her, holding her hand, alternately berating and pardoning Sam. Mattie could see even now her aunt's credulous, halfway apologetic look as she had talked to her of a recipe which had never been known to fail. It called for a cake which, when eaten, would turn wayward feet from any wandering road back to the ways of home, which would change any man, however cold, into the sweetest lover born. Mattie remembered how she shuddered when her aunt had leaned close to her, as if she were afraid that the very shadows might hear her, and had whispered into her ears the tally of the obscene ingredients of that charm. She had forbidden her aunt ever to speak to her again of that sinful cake.

Mattie did not know just how she happened to be at Madam Samantha's. She only remembered that she had not been as strong as Christ; she too had reached the point where she had cried out in agony, "My God, my God, why hast Thou forsaken me?" But (unlike her Elder Brother, she had not been able to continue, "Thy will be done." She would not let Aunt Mandy know that she had come here. Aunt Mandy would exult too much if she knew that Mattie had finally succumbed to her insistent plea that all means of redress were not confined to Mount Hebron's altar. Mattie wondered what Mrs. Brandon would have said, had she known. She would laugh, probably, and call her foolish.

As she waited in Madam Samantha's living-room, twirling the madam's card about in her hand, Mattie felt that surely one who promised so much ought to be able to do something for her. Madam Samantha's manifesto assured the identification of lost jewels, the revelation of the past, present, and future, and a happy adjustment in all affairs of the heart. As Mattie gazed about the drably furnished parlor she was relieved to find that the madam was a religious person. There was nothing here to frighten; none of the terrifying things of which she had heard and against which she had had to fortify herself before venturing into the madam's presence. There were no skulls about; nothing sinister. On the wall hung a large picture of the madam arrayed in an ample white robe, as if she were the mother superior of some religious order. There were many crosses and burning hearts and several religious prints, one of which represented the beginning of the world. God sat on a high white cloud, surveying His handiwork. He was a venerable white gentleman, but the two disembodied attendants who flew beside Him, smiling their joy at His new creation, were beautiful, curly-headed colored cherubs. Mattie felt infinitely more at ease after she had seen this picture.

When Madam Samantha entered the parlor a few moments later, Mattie was surprised and a bit disappointed to find her so simple. There was a faint kitchen odor about her, as if she had just been interrupted in the preparation of her evening meal. In the eyes of one who had not read her card and been forewarned, she might have passed as a mere housewife or cook. A plump, middle-aged brown woman, with an imperturbable face, there was no sign of magic upon her, nothing in her visage or manner that might identify her with those who behold with a more than human eye. She did not even wear her white robe.

She did not ask Mattie why she had come to her, but merely drew up a small rocking-chair and sat down, facing her client and rocking. For a moment she sat looking at Mattie as if not seeing her, as if looking beyond her and through her, with a vacuous stare on her placid, unchanging face. Her tranquillity agitated and frightened Mattie, who had been prepared for something more violent. She was not equipped to meet this ease and preci-

sion. Suddenly Madam Samantha leaned toward
Mattie and took both her hands in her own; the
mystic's hands were moist and had a greasy feel, as
if she had just taken them out of dish-water. She
closed her eyes and leaned back in her chair, still
keeping Mattie's hands in hers. Mattie could see
now that Madam Samantha's closed eyes were
twitching, as if some dormant nerve had suddenly
been galvanized into life, and she could feel an
appreciable strengthening of the grip by which
the two clammy hands entwined her own.

And now madam was speaking: "I see lights,
and lights, and lights opening up before you."
This dramatic commencement was indispensable
to Madam Samantha. Those who came to consult
her usually came in darkness, and lights were a
good omen, a symbol in which her clients could
read their eventual triumph over the evil forces
which they usually felt were working against
them.

"You are in trouble." With her eyes still closed
Madam Samantha hazarded a guess which nine
times out of ten brought a bewildered affirmation,
and bits of involuntary information which might
serve as further clues.

As Mattie inclined her head as a sign that she
had divined correctly, the mystic opened her eyes
and looked at her fully. What she saw in the drawn

black face, almost lost in the surrounding black of her funereal attire must have confirmed her thought that Mattie was a respectable person, one for whom she would hazard a strayed husband as being more likely than a lax lover.

"I see a dark man," said Madam Samantha, and the fierce grip of Mattie's hand in her own confirmed her conjecture. "And a light woman," she continued, employing a rarely failing combination. Mattie's nails sank sharply into Madam Samantha's oily palms.

The mystery-probing eyes were fluttering again. Mattie watched them roll upwardly convulsively, until she could see only a ridge of white being flayed by a frenzied lid.

"All will be well in the end," said Madam Samantha at last. She had regained her composure and seemed to have triumphed in her struggle with the spirits. "The spirits tell me that you will overcome. I see lights and lights about you." She leaned forward and smiled as if the séance were over.

Mattie felt weak and unsatisfied. It was not encouragement that she wanted. She wanted something occult and powerful, some dark, ancestral way of overcoming.

"I want him back," she heard herself saying,

sorrowfully. "I want to know some way of getting him back. I hoped you could tell me."

"I know a sure way, but it will cost you an extra dollar," admitted Madam Samantha, cautiously.

"That will be all right," said Mattie.

Madam Samantha arose and left the room for a moment. When she returned she carried a little bottle in which was a colorless liquid like water. "This water is holy," she explained, handing the phial to Mattie. "You must take something he has worn or had about him, something he has loved or cared a lot about. Sprinkle it with this water, then put it under your pillow and sleep on it. Do this for three nights' running and he will come back. I can't say how soon or how late, but he will come back."

It was a matter of rigid belief with Madam Samantha that every wanderer came back sooner or later.

That night Mattie pleaded a headache in order that she might get to her room early. She was glad when Aunt Mandy had finished fussing over her and had gone to her own room. The old lady was happy to get to bed herself; the strain of working again left her tired and spiritless.

Mattie fidgeted about, poking into drawers and into the corners of the bedroom closet, searching

for something worthy of bearing the test of bringing Sam back to her. Madam Samantha had said
it must be something he had cared a great deal
about, something he had loved. She held up a
soiled tie which she found in the closet. It was
sleazy, and frayed at the ends. She cast it aside as
unworthy. A torn handkerchief and a buttonless
shirt fell into discard with the tie.

Suddenly as her hand groped about in one of
the drawers she stopped transfixed, as if something
had nailed it there. Something that he had loved
and had had about him, Madam Samantha had
said. There was nothing that he had loved at one
time more than that on which her hand was resting. These things had been very dear to him. As
if she were bringing to light an embalmed memory, she drew forth the handkerchief. The steel
ridge of the closed razor smote her as she unloosed
the knot by which she had shut her talismans in,
while the cards rested there in a compact greasy
pack. She laid them on the bed, never taking her
eyes from them as she undressed. She found nothing strange in kneeling to pray before she carried
out Madam Samantha's instructions. As she
dropped the liquid on the cards, she agitated them
in order that the fluid might spread impartially
along the frayed edges, and in between. With a
fierce, imploring finger she smeared the razor

handle and the back of the blade with the liquid. The handkerchief had not been his; it could not aid in the charm. She folded it carefully and put it back in the drawer. She placed the razor and cards under her pillow, and climbed into bed.

Chapter Fifteen

"WAKE up, honey, and know that God do answer prayer!"

With Aunt Mandy's admonition in her ears, Mattie sat up with a start, rubbing her eyes to keep their sleep-weighted lids from falling back upon them. In the frosty twilight, outlined like a tiny harmless ghost, Aunt Mandy beamed down upon her niece, her small bright eyes snapping with excitement. Before her aunt could explain, Mattie knew. Sam had come back! And she had not slept three whole nights through on the cards and razor baptized with Madam Samantha's holy water! This would have been the third night. The charm was still underneath her pillow. And Sam had returned! As she jumped out of bed to grab up the scarlet kimona, thankful that she could welcome him back attired in this peace-offering, she wondered which had drawn him home, her prayers or Madam Samantha's charm. Now that she felt that no aid other than Heaven's was needed, she hoped that Jesus had done it all.

But it was not Sam who turned to meet her as

she rushed past Aunt Mandy into the cold parlor. She stopped short with disappointment striving with fear on her face as she saw Emma May standing there, but a different Emma May from the one whom she had gone seeking with a hatchet clutched against her bosom. That woman had been lovely with a loveliness which Mattie had resented more than her insolence, and she had been gay and defiant, with her derisive eyes mocking Mattie's pain and discomfiture. She had been strong enough to win Sam back after the baby had been born dead. But the Emma May who stood there now had been stripped of that happy animation; the round predatory hands hung listlessly at her sides; the brown eyes, heavily penciled with the deep dark rings of sleeplessness, were filmed over with nothing more challenging than worry and fear.

Emma May did not give Mattie time to speak.

"Sam's sick," she said. "He needs you."

"Did he send you for me?" Mattie steadied herself against the door, knowing it did not matter whether he had sent or not. She was his wife; for that alone her place was at his side. And more than that, wild horses couldn't have kept her away now. But it would be sweet to know that in his time of need he had turned to her, that this other woman had not been all-sufficient.

"Yes, he sent me for you," said Emma May. She seemed totally oblivious of the circumstances under which they had had their previous encounter.

All Mattie's resentment of Emma May blew over and away like smoke.

"How long has he been sick?" she called from her room, where she was dressing feverishly.

"Four days," Emma May called back. "We had a fuss at the house one night after the show was over. He couldn't forget the baby. He was always talkin' about it. That's what we was fussin' about. He got mad and ran out. When he came back in the mornin' he didn't have his coat, and couldn't tell how he'd lost it, 'cause he was stinkin' drunk, and cold right to the bone. He was shaking like a leaf. I put him to bed, and he's been there burning like a furnace ever since."

"Did you have a doctor?" Mattie already had her hat and coat on. She felt almost comradely toward Emma May as she opened the door to let her by.

"He wouldn't let me get a doctor. Said all he needed to do was to stay in bed, and that it would pass. But I don't think it will pass; he's been hackin' and spittin' blood."

They were out in the street now, and walking rapidly, close to each other, almost as if their arms were intertwined. The early-morning air stung them fiercely; it was little past one o'clock and there were few people on the street. The winter had killed all the dazzling drones.

Emma May didn't have a whole apartment. She had rented a large room and a small alcove in a private house not far from the Star Palace. The alcove served her for kitchen, while the one large room made up the deficit.

For a moment Mattie could hardly make out anything in the room after Emma May had opened the door softly and let her in. Emma May had left one light burning in the hope that Sam would feel better, and not be so lonely if there were light about him; but to keep it from being a glaring and disturbing cheerfulness she had wrapped a dark-blue handkerchief around the bulb, so that the light that was sifted through was mellow and misty.

Sam was sleeping, but battling for his breath, almost as if he had to wrench it from his disobliging body. Mattie tiptoed up to the bed, and as she looked down at him she felt like crying out aloud. It was cruel that just four days of sickness should wreak such havoc with him. These four days had wasted him more than the bearing of her baby had done her. He had been lean, to be sure, but in a hard, straight way, like a nail or a column of ebony; but he was whittled down now to a soft pliant travesty that mocked the withdrawal of all his strength. He was no more than a caricature of himself as he lay there, his cheeks so sunken that she felt that they must be touching inside his mouth; and his lips, which had never been full, were now so slack and loose, and so fallen away from his teeth as to be grotesque.

She leaned down and touched him, but almost drew her hand back in fright as it burned beneath the scaly dry heat of his forehead. She was so close to him that she could see how the fever had routed away all the jet-black sleekness of his skin, leaving it dry and ashy. She wanted to weep. He opened his eyes and looked at her, and they were the only beauty about him which had not been violated. They were still brilliant and dynamic, the finest eyes she had ever seen. He looked at her for a moment as if she were a stranger. And then in his weakness and sleepy sickness he struck her by calling her "Emma May."

"It isn't Emma, Sam. It's Mattie." She corrected him gently and without reproof.

"How'd you know I was sick, Mattie?" His eyes fluttered up in painful surprise, and his low striving voice was devoid of any expectation. Mattie looked up quickly at Emma May, who was standing near by, still wearing her hat and coat as if she were lost in her own room, or a stranger who had just chanced in. Emma May threw out her hands in a half-weary, half-defiant gesture, and turned away.

So Sam had not sent for her at all; not even in his sickness had he felt a need of her. Emma May had simply come to her as a last resource, because Emma May was tired and worn out and of no use to him while he was sick. But even for this half a loaf Mattie was grateful, glad to be near him even in another woman's house, even at another woman's behest.

"Emma May came for me," she said, stroking his head.

"It was good of you to come, Mattie."

"It was my duty," she said, simply, but he knew it was more.

"Hadn't we better get you a doctor, Sam?" Mattie was anxious now, and filled with a deep fear of the time lost, during which he had been allowed to lie there undoctored, as if his malady would eat itself away and so cure him. She made as if to get up, but his pitifully wasted black hand reached out to deny her.

" 'Tain't no need to hurry now," he said. "How's A'nt Mandy?"

"Well, Sam, and missing you."

"Good old A'nt Mandy." He coughed his admiration out with a sudden spasm that frightened her.

Seated on a trunk near the window, Emma May seemed to have forgotten them. Her eyes were closed, and her head was leaning against the wall as if she were too exhausted to move an inch farther. Mattie was sorry for her, and grateful, too, that she had stayed by Sam and had ministered to him so long. But the righteous flame that burned in her bosom, the flame which Sam himself had enkindled, would give her no peace.

"Don't you think I'd better send for Reverend Drummond, Sam?" She hoped he wouldn't be angry at the suggestion, but she had her duty to do. She had his soul to think of.

"What good can he do me, Mattie?" She could sense a soft irony in the low-pitched question.

"He could pray for you, Sam."

"Can't you do that, Mattie, if you think it will do any good?"

Kneeling down at the bed, she kept his hand in hers while she unbosomed herself to that God whom he had taught her to know, not knowing Him himself. She poured out in all the confidence and assurance of the simple the weight of her overburdened heart. Her voice overcame Emma May's strong snoring, and fell on Sam's ears like a far-away and pleasant music. He heard nothing of what she was saying, but her hand in his was like a sedative seeping through his skin. When she had finished and rose up, slipping her hand away, he stirred and looked at her sheepishly. "I'm afraid I went to sleep," he apologized.

"That doesn't matter, Sam. It's good if you can sleep." She drew a chair up softly beside the bed. "Try to sleep again, I'll sit here beside you and watch."

She sat there quietly for a while half frightened by the queerness of the situation in which she found herself ministering to her husband in another woman's home. Emma May had abandoned them entirely in the blessedness of repose. Sam lay with his eyes contrarily open now, watching Mattie with a strange childish happiness in his eyes. Suddenly he beckoned her to lean close to him, as if he wanted to tell her something secretly, something he had just thought of.

"Mattie, you're a grand woman," was what she heard as she leaned over him, praise enough to set all the bells of heaven ringing for her, and to charge her eyes with tears. She could only pat his hand. The tribute had cost him a spasm of pain.

"I'd like to go home," he continued. Mattie's heart leaped at the thought that she would not have to sleep on her charm again. But she tried to persuade him to wait until morning. It was too late, she told him, to disturb himself now. She would sit there beside him until morning came; then she would take him home. But he became querulous and insistent, hacking and spitting blood, until she had to wake Emma May to tell her that she was taking him home, and to ask for his clothes. Emma May accepted the news with the lassitude of complete defeat, and even with an alacrity which Mattie thought unkind and disproportionate with Sam's worth. Emma May brought the clothes and laid them on the bed. Then, as if some sudden inner delicacy whispered to her, she stepped into the alcove that formed her kitchen, drawing the curtain after her and shutting herself off from Mattie and Sam.

Sam, his whole body in a tumult of fever, was pitifully weak, unable to stand alone, and Mattie had to dress him in bed. When she had finished dressing him she had to ask Emma May to help her get him downstairs. They found a taxi with an amiable young fellow glad of a fare and willing to aid her in getting him home.

"I'll send for his other clothes," said Mattie as she got into the taxi, and she wondered if she ought to ask Emma May to come to the house. But she thought better of it. If Emma May came she would not deny her, but she could not bring her-

self to invite Sam's woman to her home. She felt
sad for Emma May going back to her empty room.

Aunt Mandy welcomed the wanderer back with
a loud, raucous geniality that seemed strange coming from her elfin throat, and he tried to laugh
back at her in the old happy way, but the pain
throttled the laughter in him and made him clutch
his side with a short, low whistle. Mattie undressed him and put him into their bed again, and
neither knowing nor caring whether the results
might be dangerous, she climbed in with him, to
fall asleep with his scorching body locked in her
arms.

Dr. Brandon said it was pneumonia the next
morning, double, and with pleurisy. In a brisk
professional tone he gave her instructions about
binding Sam's side to keep the water from rising,
and then he told her that there was little cause to
hope for Sam's recovering. He could not put up a
good fight; he had held nothing back in living,
and there was no reserve now on which he could
draw. Liquor had torn down every defense. Dr.
Brandon said he was sorry for her, and if there
was anything he and Mrs. Brandon could do, she
had but to call on them.

When the doctor had gone, Sam wanted to know
what he had said, and she told him that the doctor
had ordered quiet and plenty of air, and had said

that he would pull through. But her simulated gaiety could not deceive him, nor override the wisdom of those who are about to die. He looked at her quietly, and lay unstirring, lost in the few thoughts he could wrench away from the sharp, stabbing pains in his side. He asked her to lift his head a little; it hurt so much to breathe.

All day he lay silent and ebbing, coughing bright clots of blood into the handkerchief which Mattie held to his lips. Aunt Mandy, who had stayed home to help Mattie, brought him a bit of chicken broth which Mattie tried to feed him with a spoon, but it pained him to swallow.

He fell into a heavy doze with Mattie's hand cooling his parched forehead. When he awoke it was evening, dark in his room, and he could hear Mattie and Aunt Mandy talking in the room next to his. He lay still, shamming with the sly trickery of the sick who feel that things are being kept from them.

"He's going, Aunt Mandy. Dr. Brandon told me so."

There were several hard, rhythmic beats of a rocking-chair before he heard Aunt Mandy reply, "We all got to go some day."

"I know that, Aunt Mandy, but that don't make it any easier for me. I could stand it a little better if I knew how he was going. He's been out of church so long. But if there was some way of knowing that he was going to be saved, I could go on living and hope to meet him and my baby some day."

In the bedroom the sick man almost laughed aloud. As if there could be any meeting afterwards, any place, between them and that little black baby that hadn't lived an hour!

"Sometimes there is a way of knowing," Aunt Mandy's voice floated in to him like something veiled and insidious, something not of the earth.

"How do you mean, Aunt Mandy?" Sam felt as if he could see Mattie sitting out there, leaning closer to her aunt, her sleek black face shining with a desire to know.

"Sometimes God sends us visions. To the ones what's been good and believing, and what's served Him all their days, He sends a sign. When my mother died we knew for sure where she was going, because she cried out that there was lights shining all around her, and music, singing, and her own mother who'd been dead twenty years came and stood at the bed all dressed in white. But if you're going to be lost ——"

"What then, Aunty?"

What then, indeed? What other fairy tale was that old woman out there going to tell Mattie? Sam braced himself to keep from moving. It was funny to be dying like this with these old darky superstitions ringing in his ears.

"If you're going to be lost, you still has visions, but of another kind. It gets dark and you can't see with your eyes wide open, and sometimes the devil himself comes for you like a big black bat or a snake." The old lady was enjoying herself. This was the proper talk for a death-room, and her rocker beat a sweet, complacent cadence as she went on." There was a family at my home in the South, so bad that every one of them went to the devil, mother, father, and son. They still talk about the Higginses where I come from. They was always drinking and fighting and cussing, and they never darkened the door of the church. The mother died first, and with her last breath she told old man Higgins she would scratch his eyes out in hell. The son Ike died with his boots on. A man caught him with his wife, and ripped his stomach open. Old man Higgins let the county bury the boy and never even went to the funeral. But when *he* died, they say a little coal-black man with one eye in his head danced down from the attic with chains dangling behind him, singing, 'If you're ready, old Higgins, let's go.' And folks say that on the outside of the house his wife and his son Ike stood, three times their natural size, ready to show him the way to hell."

The old lady paused for breath, and there was silence for a while to be broken finally by Mattie's querulous, anxious voice: "I'd like so much to know. I'd give my life to be sure he was saved. Maybe I'd better send for Reverend Drummond, anyhow."

Sam had a sudden panicky feeling. He didn't want Reverend Drummond. If he were going to die, he wanted to die in peace. Even now, on his dying pallet, he didn't believe any more than he had believed the night he looked through the slits of his fingers at Mattie at Mount Hebron Church, no more than he had believed the first night he had tricked God with his cards and razor. His way had been the best for him, and there was nothing the preacher could add or take away. He had enjoyed living and loving, and what was there to fear in dying? All his life he had played tricks, and when he had been caught the troubled preacher had not denounced him. That evangelist had been swell. Now one more trick was left him, the sweetest, kindest trick of all, to keep Mattie from too much weeping, and to ease her simple, believing soul. For Mattie would go on believing and going to church. She would never get the benefit of her beauty, never sow it wildly and reap a whirlwind of passion. She would never go off with another man as he had done with Emma May. With an infinite pity he thought of his cards and his razor, so rotten a base for such a good woman to build her life on. And she would go on and on believing in them, and he would be dead and buried and she would tell over and over how he had saved her, and never know that it had been a trick. But one more trick now while this steady tightening in his throat was still loose enough to let him speak, a sweet trick to set at ease the mind of this good woman who loved him, and who still in his dying had no thought except for what she called his soul.

The bed creaked as he turned, and before he could call her, Mattie was there at his side. It was so dark that he could only see her eyes and the polished arc of her teeth.

"I was sleeping," he said, "but the music woke me up."

"Music, Sam? What music? There hasn't been any music." Her credulity had not yet snapped at the deceptive hook he was dangling before her.

"Oh yes, there was music, the sweetest kind ever," he insisted. "And why have you got the lights on so soon? They seem brighter than ever; they almost hurt my eyes."

He heard her suck her breath in sharply, and he saw the dark outline of her hand rise and clutch her breast; she was caught, thoroughly ensnared.

She turned from him and fled to the door, where she called for Aunt Mandy. The old lady came running.

"Tell Aunt Mandy, Sam, tell her what you told me." Mattie could scarcely get the words out; she leaned above him, breathless and staring, made more comely by her belief in this sign of redemption. Aunt Mandy stood mystified at the foot of the bed.

"Prop me up, Mattie; it's hard breathing." He thought of an old song he used to sing, "Turn me over on my left side, 'cause my right side hurts me so."

Then when her arm had eased him up on the pillow so that the demon in his throat seemed to subside a little, he told Aunt Mandy, "There was such sweet music, singing, and playing like I never heard before. And I asked Mattie to turn the light down a little. It's so bright it hurts my eyes."

He could feel Mattie's hand tremble on his forehead. Aunt Mandy stood transfixed and mute. He knew that for them he was forever saved.

During the night the demon clogged his windpipe completely. Mattie had slept on a couch in the front room at Dr. Brandon's suggestion. She found him cold, and suddenly handsome again. Remembering that he had heard music and seen lights, she did not weep loudly as she desired to do, but she sorrowed decently, with quiet tears. She would tell Reverend Drummond how he had died that he might know that he could truthfully preach him saved. She would invite Emma May to the funeral.

THE END